A Very Merlin Christmas

Part four of the lost Merlin chronicles
by Toby Vennard

A quick note from the author

Dedicated to my sons Noah and Todd and my Mum and Dad (the real Nanny Vicky and Grandad Barry), and not forgetting Noah and Todd's real cousin James. This is of course for all children out there, as should be the true nature of Christmas. Saint Nicholas is considered to be the patron saint of children which is why being Santa Claus / Father Christmas / Saint Nick / Papa Noel and all the other names children know him by, is the perfect vocation for him, even if you don't believe in him, hopefully after reading this book you will start to at the very least begin to believe in the spirit of Christmas itself, perfectly captured in the book 'a Christmas carol' by Charles Dickens, one of my all time favourites! Without wishing to give away too many spoilers before you've started reading this book, perhaps a mention/dedication to Tiny Tim, the young Cratchit boy who features in this book too, but I'll let you find that out for yourselves.

Hand-drawn illustrations ©2021 Lorna Cameron-Burnett. All other imagery including the front cover ©2023 Toby Vennard - using AI image generating software.

Chapter One

This book continues after the (at the time of writing this) famously missing 3rd instalment of the lost Merlin Chronicles entitled "Reality roulette". If you are lucky enough to read the missing instalment one day in your own future or you happen to know of its whereabouts, it may help with any confusion, and indeed you can ignore this first paragraph. I will attempt to fill in any detail so far discovered to help. Reading the 2nd instalment, 'Ghost writers' may help to save confusion over references to characters which without the 2nd book might not make sense.

What we do know so far is that Merlin left with Dan his trusty dragon to go back to the early 16th century, to visit his old friend Michel Nostradamus in Provence in the South of France, to try to find a better understanding of the universe and it's many mysteries and indeed the eternal mystery of man's reason for being a part of it and what happens in the afterlife, if there is one?

Merlin went to find Dan down by the caves they had discovered together upon their arrival, to find Dan had once again fallen asleep, presumably after his long flight to Provence in the South of France and indeed 400 years into the past courtesy of his amazing magical master. Merlin approached his pet quietly, being careful not to startle him but also to enjoy walking through the cool water of the stream leading up to the cave entrance. Merlin reached for Dan's left ear and began to softly rub it. Dan was already aware of his master's presence but was too tired to acknowledge him so continued to pretend to be asleep, until he mustered enough energy to mutter the following words in a deep but soft grumble and with a minimum of movement from his mouth,

"Hello, Master, I do apologise, I'm quite sleepy, I will be with you shortly, if you need to say anything, I can hear you and as you can hear, I am capable of responding".

"Hello you wonderful beast, I hope I have not been too long, you'll be pleased to know 'mission accomplished'! and when and only when you are ready I am now ready to return to England and the 21st century", Merlin said.

"Okay", Dan mumbled sleepily, "give me time to go drink from the lake and I'll start trying to wake myself up".

"Agreed!"

"Ok, stand back".

Merlin did so at which point, Dan opened one eye, managed to raise himself up as far as the height of the cave entrance to allow and then treat himself to a long stretch of his back legs further into the cave, his front legs stretched out impressively in front of him and he yawned the biggest yawn Merlin had ever seen, even from Dan. Dan breathed in, which made him cough, sending a large fireball with black smoke out of the cave and into the air. He then shuffled forward making his way out into the warm Mediterranean air and made his way to the lake by the caves, he was thirsty and in need of a dip in the cool water. After which he turned to face his master who was waiting patiently by the cave entrance.

"Right", Dan announced, shaking off the water from his body like a very large dog, "let's do this!"

"Good lad", said Merlin, " 21st century England, here we come!".

Dan lowered his head and a front leg to allow Merlin to climb on to his back, which he duly did. The pair flew high into the air. Like before, Merlin raised one hand (the other hanging onto Dan for dear life, and said the incantation that would allow them to jump ahead in time. A feint (but visible enough for Dan), large golden ring had appeared in the sky in front of them, Dan headed straight for it and flew through. To the untrained eye, nothing had changed, but they were flying over the sea. The real giveaway that anything had worked was when a nearby plane carrying dumbfounded passengers and its captain and crew missed them by an uncomfortably close distance causing turbulence for both the plane and for Dan. Merlin had never experienced this sensation before but as soon as Dan lifted his head to ensure his passenger was okay, Merlin reached forward and gave Dan a reassuring rub of his left ear shouting the words "Carry on , lad, make for the apple tree above Marlborough, you've more than earned an 'all you can eat' feast!".

Dan didn't need telling twice he leaned into the wind to try and streamline himself to go faster, he adored those apples, and had spent years resisting visiting the tree multiple times as his Master had asked him, so when he was told he was allowed free reign over it, he flew as fast as he could, reaching the southern shores of England in record time. Merlin remembered to wave in the direction of Bognor Regis as they flew over Sussex. He had remembered Noah and Todd telling him all about their grandparents who lived there near the pier. They flew North and West through Hampshire, part of Berkshire and on to Wiltshire, following the M4 motorway as a reference to their position. An excited Dan plummeted towards the apple tree but skillfully landed so as not to hurt his Master, but quickly enough so that he could get on with making short work of collecting apples. The landing had not gone entirely unnoticed. A nearby farmer, out on his tractor, pulled up alongside a nearby gate between the fields and stood scratching his head and occasionally rubbing his eyes in disbelief while watching a dragon munching a tree. 'The lads down the Baker's arms are never gonna believe this when I tell 'em later', he thought to himself. He didn't want to raise attention that he'd seen them so the farmer stepped off the tractor and made the decision to make his way back home on foot, he would pick the tractor up later.

Chapter Two

"Don't forget to spit the pips out, we might get more trees growing that way. More trees means more apples!" said Merlin, picking up a few himself for his bag, maybe a few in the hood of his cloak. Something that would have been unavailable to him if he'd stayed in the clothes Will had given him back in Marlborough. After a decent feast, Dan and Merlin flew back to Dan's cave where all the cave dwelling animals were waiting for them with the notable exception of Mollie and Poem the two owls, who were still recovering from their recent change in daily routine, and were using this time to sleep so hopefully this way they could visit Noah and Todd again like they had done for a long time now. The animals made sure they stayed to one side to give Dan some landing room. Another perfect landing. Merlin climbed off Dan and said hello to the gathered crowd of animals, there always seemed to be more than before. Including, Kevin the kestrel who had flown to freedom from a nearby falconry centre just inside Oxfordshire. He had spotted Dan and Merlin earlier so flew ahead to tell the rest of the gang which is how they knew to be outside waiting for their imminent arrival.

"Hello everyone, "Dan rumbled.

Everyone replied with 'Welcome back', 'great to see you', 'how was the journey'?

"I shall come inside and tell you all about it", said Dan, starting to back himself into the cave entrance, after he got comfortable he gently woke the two owls that he found napping on a large stone. If only to warn them that he was going to light the fireplace he had fashioned in the far wall of the main part of the cave. The two owls promptly stood up, shook their feathers after a good stretch and made their way into a little nook nearby. Dan did a quick scan to make sure there were no small unsuspecting animals or indeed humans anywhere inside. He started to make a rumbling sound and then blew out a steady stream of fire towards the fireplace. There was a decent amount of kindling in there from before so a fire took hold well. The animals all started to enter the cave once more and the two owls emerged from their nook, taking up a place to lay down on a nearby ledge. They all waited eagerly for Dan to tell them all about his travels and adventure with Merlin. Meanwhile Merlin had begun walking in the direction of Marlborough to try and catch up with Zoe and Chris. It was a clear, crisp autumn afternoon which was very agreeable. Just as he got near the road into town, he heard a familiar sound. It was Will on his motorbike with Bertha hanging on as tight as she could, sat on the back, they were also on the way to the house behind Marlborough college. Merlin was looking forward to catching up with people and finding out how things were going in Oxford with all the amazing people and indeed family members he had met previously. A very pleasant stroll put Merlin in Marlborough, a little before supper time. He walked up to the familiar door of his distant family and knocked, excited to see who would answer. First of all came the sound of Harvey, their large dog barking to tell anyone inside that there were people wanting the door opening and also to let everyone outside know that he was guarding the house, so there was to be no tricky business, because as the family dog it was his duty to protect everyone inside. All dogs have this regardless of if they're a small dog like a teacup chihuahua called Princess and lives their best life in their owner's handbag. They will put so much effort into barking that all four feet will leave the ground with each bark. Whereas something the size of Harvey which was like a small bear, needed very little effort to leave the visitor with absolutely no doubt in their mind that if they put one foot out of turn, they will be taken down and made to explain themselves, and potentially seen off the premises or, at the very least, if it's a large but affectionate breed like a labrador, you stand the risk of being licked to death, regardless of breed, they will bark at quite literally anything, people they know,people they don't know such as the postman, inanimate objects because they feel they're being stared at, other dogs, thin air, people that are known or unknown but are walking past the house on the other side of the road but are within range of the house. Eventually, a woman's voice was heard. It was Zoe.

"Shut up, Harvey, go to your bed, before I kick you so hard

you'll end up through the window and out in the garden where you'll stay! Oh come here, " her voice softened, as she gave Harvey a hug and ruffled his fur, "Mummy doesn't mean it, she could never hurt you, my baby, just go to your bed and chill out for a bit, it's not your job to protect us you big softy".

Zoe then pulled herself up to her full height, Let out an exasperated breath, shouted towards the front door, "I'm just on my way, won't be a second", walked to the door, opened it to see Merlin standing there with a wide grin on his face. Harvey's face suddenly appeared next to Zoe's legs. Merlin reached forward to greet him.

"Oh hello again, Merlin, come on in, this fluffy maniac won't stop barking without reason, but he knows you so he should be okay".

"Of course he will, won't ya, lad, I saw Will and Bertha coming up the road just a short while ago." Merlin replied.

"Yes they're upstairs I think I can hear them walking about, no doubt they'll be down soon enough, "Zoe turned towards the stairs and shouted up, "Bertha? Will? Visitor!".

"Okay!" came the reply from both of them. Merlin went into the living room and made himself comfortable.

"Apple juice, Merlin?" came Zoe's voice from the kitchen.

"Please!" Merlin replied.

After a few moments Will and Bertha appeared from the kitchen having taken that diversion from the stairs to fetch themselves some drinks and raid the fridge for some sort of snack.

"Dad!" Bertha exclaimed, "so good to see you, I wasn't sure if you were around still, or where you might be to be honest" she said, handing Merlin his drink.

"Hello, darling girl, you're looking well, and young Will, how's you, lad?" Merlin asked.

Will reached forward and shook Merlin's hand. "Very good thanks, Bertie and I haven't been back long, we decided to leave Katy to it for the weekend, I'll take Bertie back again for next week. How are things? Been up to much since we last saw you? Did you find your friend?"

"Yes indeed, Dan and I went back to 16th century Provence, found Nostradamus and a few others, got some interesting information there, then we flew back earlier today, nearly got hit by a plane en route, a charming flight over Sussex, Hampshire and bits of Berkshire. All very pretty from the air". Always glad to be back on solid ground though".

Will sat next to Bertha, the two held hands.

"So", Merlin continued, " how is everyone back in Oxford? I was so sorry to leave in such a hurry, I did so enjoy getting to know everyone.

"Mostly everyone is still there, " Bertha took hold of the conversation, she felt she could probably fill her Dad in on events better as Will tended to add more detail than was needed, and let his mind wander onto other things too much. "We reckon Sam is still in a bit of shock over the whole pub thing, but he's dealing well with it, it's stuffed with ghosts every night. Will has yet to come up with a way of them enjoying a drink rather than it all simply pouring straight through them".

"I must admit I'm at a bit of a brick wall with that one".

"Anyone new and interesting made themselves known?"

"Well lots of 'new' because news of recent events have spread through the afterlife like a disease. Not even John and Jack can identify a lot of them".

"Brilliant!" Merlin exclaimed, "I shall have to make another visit soon! How about the family? Any more news with them?".

"No, Katy's Mum and Nan returned home but we all agreed to stay in touch in whatever form that takes. Katy has come to terms with what her future has in store for her, I think she was a bit overwhelmed what with finding out 'the' Merlin is her grandson and all that".

"Indeed, I found the whole thing both overwhelming but fascinating, it's a rare event to be able to meet people in your family going back four generations, wonderful really, a truly savoured moment".

"What are your next plans then , Merlin?" asked Will.

"Good question, nothing occurs to me straight off, but that's the joy of being able to meet so many people across time. Adventure and things that need sorting tend to find me without me really having to do anything, so we shall see, in the meantime, I shall spend my time between here, Swindon and Oxford I imagine".

"Oh while I think of it, Merlin, " came Zoe's voice as she walked in from the kitchen, "this letter arrived for you!".

"For me? How in the world does anyone know I'm here?"

"I suggest you open it and find out".

Merlin examined the envelope for clues, the handwriting was unnervingly familiar but not enough that he could identify it. There were no postmarks and indeed no stamp, so the original location wasn't known. He carefully opened the envelope and retrieved the paper from inside. Clearly not carefully enough as a modest amount of glitter fell out of it all over Merlin's lap. This made Harvey let out a single very loud bark, Merlin opened the letter and immediately looked for the sender's name, usually at the end and their address normally at the top,

"Well, that's unlikely. I'm not a fan of the word impossible as everyone is aware, apparently this letter is from me to myself. Forgive me while I read a moment, " Bertha and Will watched Merlin for subtle clues as to the content of the letter by way of body language and reaction. They didn't have to wait long before Merlin let out a very loud "Ha!", Harvey let out an uncharacteristically small whimper so Will and Bertha made a fuss of him, choosing not to interrupt Merlin's train of thought by asking what caused his amusing outburst. After a short while, Merlin folded the letter and put it back in it's envelope.

"Well, " Merlin continued, "there's a turn up. I told you this time travel malarky caused adventure to follow me around. The letter is actually from me, which makes sense, if anyone's going to know where I am, it's me. I need to follow a few instructions from myself, but essentially I need to gather a few bits, a few people potentially a dragon and get over to Swindon".

Zoe had been listening in, "I can run you over there, Merlin, Chris is over there at the moment, visiting Dave".

"So that's where Dad is, I was wondering about that, "Will chipped in, "also, Merlin, you're back in your old clothes, which suggests you've been back here at some point before today?"

"Yes, indeed, I came here after visiting Dan in his cave and stayed over the night before travelling to France", Merlin confirmed. "Ok, Zoe, that would fab, I'm obviously ready any time you are.

Question, if Chris is already over there, what car are you going to use?"

"Oh, yes, luckily I have my own car so that Chris and I have our independence when needed. Will has his bike, so I suggest if you and I take my car and throw Harvey in the back, the boys would never forgive me for leaving him alone or indeed not taking him over there. Will and Bertha can whizz over on the bike if they want to join us, or maybe they want to stay here, up to them, again with independence". Bertha squeezed Will's hand as if to say "Don't worry I've got this.".

"Don't worry about us, Zoe we dropped in on them all earlier, we figured it wasn't very out of the way on our way back, but do keep us updated with everything, Dad".

"Okay then", Zoe replied, "well, no time like the present, Merlin, Harvey, follow me".

They left by the front door. Zoe's car was parked out the front of the house. Zoe pointed her key fob at the bright green car sat across the road, pressed a button on the fob which caused the indicators to flash, the mirrors to unfold to the correct position and a variety of courtesy lights both inside and outside the car to illuminate. Another button made the boot of the car to pop open and lift the tailgate which was Harvey's signal to jump in the back. Zoe and Merlin climbed in the front.

"Now, " Zoe started, "this will be a new experience for you,

Chapter Three

Merlin, this car is electric, by which I mean it doesn't use combustible fuels, it simply gets charged using electricity and stores that energy in batteries under the floor".

"How extraordinary", Merlin stated, "does it fly?"

"No, I'm afraid not, but it's quite quick so won't take us long to get over to Swindon, are you comfortable?"

"Yes thank you, very!"

"Excellent". Zoe started pressing various buttons and bringing up various displays on the two screens in front of them,"right, car is on, just got to turn around, this little bit out the front here is one way".

"When you say the car is on, I don't hear the engine?"

"That's because there isn't one, it uses an electric motor instead, meaning it's virtually silent".

As they drove back past the house they caught sight of Bertha and Will waving from the front door and waved back. Zoe drove her and Merlin over to Swindon to see Gwen, Dave and the boys. Todd was first to spot the green car out the kitchen window, he knew this meant there would be a Harvey or at least there had better be! He ran out of the house and was greeted by Zoe with her arms out wide ready for a hug. Todd ran straight into her arms.

"Hello little man, do you want to press the special button?" Zoe asked.

"Yes please, Auntie Zoe" came the reply, Todd grabbed the key fob, pressed the *special* button and watched the tailgate lift and a big mountain of fluff jump out.

"Harvey!" Todd and Harvey moved towards each other and hugged then ran indoors together. They were a blur as they passed Noah in the hallway Noah made his way out for Auntie Zoe and Merlin of course.

"Come on Merlin, I'll get you an apple juice, what would you like, Auntie Zoe?"

"Oooh, I might have the same if there's enough?"

"Of course there is!" Noah laughed, remembering the sheer amount of apples acquired on their last trip up to the tree. Everyone was now indoors except Harvey who was in the garden giving Hubert the hedgehog a wide berth, remembering the unfortunate incident from a previous visit. The two sat and chatted but observed what looked like their best attempt at social distancing, ie 2 metres apart but without face masks obviously. For anyone confused, social distancing was introduced in the year 2020 when a dangerous disease caused a worldwide pandemic and because it was airborne, everyone was advised not to get too close to one another."Gwen?" Zoe asked, "No sign of Chris?"

"No, should there have been?" came the reply.

"Last he told me was that he was coming here to see Dave about something, hmmm, didn't pass him on the way here, wonder where he's got to".

"How did it go, Merlin, did you find Nostra-whatshisface?" Noah asked.

"Nostradamus!" Merlin replied "Yes I did indeed, very interesting trip, found out many things! Talking of trips, Dave and Gwen, I need to talk to you about borrowing the boys, only I have another trip that needs doing and it's important that the boys join me. I promise they will be looked after, fed, watered etcetera, there will be no danger on this particular trip."

"Well, "Gwen was a little lost for words, "we trust you, of course, but perhaps if one of us came with you just in terms of having another adult to help? What do you think, Dave?"

"Yes, could do, I'm happy to help of course".

"I meant me, you'd be okay on your own here wouldn't you? I mean you've got Zoe and Chris just up the road…"

"Yes yes, " Dave interrupted, "I will be absolutely fine, of course I will, plus which if this adventure involves time travel, then I won't notice how long you're away for, it'll be a matter of hours at most, right Merlin?"

"You've got the idea Dave, We would return to the day we left", Merlin confirmed. "At least we would certainly try!".

"When are you thinking of going?" asked Zoe.

"Well, time is somewhat irrelevant seeing as we have control over it, though I must admit I'm rather keen to crack on, " Merlin replied.

"We must remember ," Gwen interrupted, "that the boys still have school, but if like you say we'll be returning to the here and now then it shouldn't be a problem".

"Indeed, if we aim for a weekend anyway it should then give us a wider margin for error in terms of getting the timing right, though I'm better at that than getting us back to the right place geographically, I'm improving though, "Merlin said with a twinkle in his eye.

"Oh, " Gwen suddenly said after suddenly remembering, " it can't be this weekend, we have family visiting".

"Oh? your side or Dave's?" Merlin asked.

"Dave's"

"Don't suppose there are any children joining us?"

"Er, yes, there's James, he's the same age as Noah".

"Brilliant, I wonder if we might be able to take him on our adventure too?"

"Well, that's up to his Mum and Dad, you'll have to ask them about that". Gwen replied.

"Fair enough, this weekend you say? Might I be able to stay here until then? Then I'm already in the right place, and a lot nearer to the others in Oxford, I fancy trying one of those bus contraptions at some point, just for the experience. I thoroughly enjoyed our trip to London that time. No offence to you Zoe of course, I enjoyed our trip here in your little green electric wonder and Dave, it was an honour to share the road with you in the marvellous Tabitha and indeed Henrietta and who can forget the unique experience of ripping through Wiltshire on the back of young Will's motorbike? I certainly can't!"

"Merlin? "Gwen began, "You're starting to ramble, you haven't offended anyone, you're family," To which Zoe nodded in agreement. In fact at that moment Dave could be heard upstairs sorting out the spare room / his study. "I would take that as a sign of Dave's approval,

" Gwen continued, "do you have everything with you that you need or is there anything at Zoe's?".

"No, no I have everything in this bag that I could possibly need, the only thing I have left behind in that direction is my dragon, I'll be needing to collect him for our adventure apparently".

"Apparently?"

"So, picture the scene, I'm sat in the living room in Marlborough when suddenly Zoe announces I've received a letter, I couldn't figure who would know I was there, turned out it was me!"

"I don't follow", said Gwen.

"I mean the letter was from me to myself, I obviously remembered where I was at the point I returned from France, so it's good to know my mind is still in relatively good working order. I'm still a bit mystified about the glitter though, I have a theory on it, but all will become clear soon I'm sure".

"Glitter?"

"Yes some fell out the envelope when I took the letter out, most odd, I can't imagine any situation where I would include glitter or any sort of decoration in any of my communications unless it was a deliberate clue, here have a look". Merlin fetched the letter out of his pocket and handed it to Gwen. As Gwen carefully or at least tried to carefully remove the letter from the envelope, enough glitter fell out to suggest the envelope had been refilled. Gwen read the letter to herself, occasionally mumbling or making little "ooooh" noises to herself.

"It even mentions the boys by name, I suppose being from you, Merlin, it would. How are you supposed to know where the other you is?" Gwen asked.

"Oh that's easy, "Merlin replied, "I've figured a way to track myself already, not that I have done so yet".

"I know exactly where you'll be!" Todd declared, shoving his hand in to an open bag of giant chocolate buttons.

"No you don't!" Noah insisted.

"Yes, I do!!" Todd barked back, "it's obvious!" Noah rolled his eyes and shook his head which Todd ignored and continued to divulge his theory, "So, let's look at the evidence, first, the glitter, hmm, I'll come back to that, the letter says it's important to bring children, not sure why us specifically, but awesome anyway. So my idea is, that Merlin will be in the North pole because children and glitter to my mind equals Christmas! And as everyone knows, the North pole have their own mailing department because they need to cope with all the incoming letters for Santa and anything outgoing will include a little piece of Christmas with it, in this case glitter. I assume their post office is run by elves as well as everything else, so they would include glitter with all correspondence in the same way all presents come with a wrap around bow or one of those stick on bows".

Noah turned slowly towards Todd with a look of disbelief . "Todd, that was epic, who are you? What have you done with my brother?".

"What do you mean? It's only a guess, He could be inside the moon? There's bound to be glitter up there, it's got to come from somewhere!"

"Brilliant, Todd, " Merlin added, "I do hope you're right, for several reasons! Tell you what we'll see if we can track other me together boys. It will be much easier at night".

Both boys were very excited by this and started to make plans for what they would say to Santa if Todd was right. Noah pointed out that Christmas wasn't very far away now so a Christmas wish list wouldn't be seen as out of place or rude to deliver in person. That evening just happened to be takeaway night in this particular house, a quick poll led to a mostly even choice between Chinese and Pizza. Merlin was perfectly happy to sample whatever was decided on, the adults all agreed on Chinese, Noah and Todd wanted Pizza, so as usual, Dave caved and agreed to do both. The boys got a large pizza to share and some garlic bread, obviously. A large selection of Chinese food arrived at the same time. Merlin soon decided dumplings were his favourite and anything concerning satè sauce. It was a Friday night so no school the next day. Despite their cousin visiting tomorrow the boys were allowed to stay up a bit later than normal. Gwen was of the opinion that, what with the excitement of impending adventure and Merlin visiting, there was no point in them going to bed at a regular time.

"When are we going to do the tracking thing, Merlin?" Noah asked.

"Well, My idea currently is to wait until your cousin James arrives as it may serve as the perfect way to introduce him to me so that he can see who I am and what I do, if that makes sense, only I don't want to scare the lad off by having time travel be his first experience, he's got a lot to catch up with, including a talking dragon!"

"He'll be fine, Merlin, "Gwen assured him, "he's just like our two, should be fun for him".

Merlin felt more settled from Gwen's words, certainly enough to tuck in to another chicken skewer.

"Now boys, remember, if you can't get through that pizza it's not a problem, all this food including the pizza can be reheated through again and eaten tomorrow", Gwen said, smiling.

The boys were given permission to get down from the table and get comfortable on the understanding they went and got washed and changed into whatever they were going to bed in. They were both back suspiciously fast, but were visibly clean and smelled that way too. With a suspicious smugness, Noah made himself comfortable on the sofa while Todd lounged on Harvey who had made himself comfortable in front of the fireplace.

Merlin was installed on a nice armchair while everyone else took root on either the sofa or grabbed a chair from the dining table. Gwen decided to sit on the floor with Todd and Harvey. Merlin shuffled and turned to his audience and announced, "I have an idea! With the fact Dave's family are due to visit tomorrow and I want to be here for that, come Sunday or even Monday, I plan, if possible, to travel to Oxford by bus, thoughts?"

"I can answer all that I reckon, " Dave interrupted. "I received a message from young James' Mum, my cousin, to say that because James' Dad can't join them tomorrow, James' Mum will be bringing him by train to visit, so I shall pop along to pick them up. And Merlin, I believe you need the S6 bus to get to Oxford from here, I can drop you off where you need to pick that up, we'll look on the internet later and work out timings for where and when you want to be there and indeed sort your return itinerary".

"Marvellous, many thanks for your help".

"Right, Gwen began, "Noah and Todd, if we have a James tomorrow, I think it's bedtime.

Todd put his entire weight on Harvey pushing all the air out of him and stood up in front of Merlin. He looked at him with his hypnotically big eyes and said, "Merrrrrlin?"

"Yeeeeees....?" Merlin replied knowing full well what was coming next.

"Um......story?" Todd asked, wearing his trademark cheeky grin.

"Certainly, I'll be up in just a moment."

"Yaaaaaaaaaaaaaaaaaaay" could be heard from both the boys as they ran upstairs.

Merlin turned to Gwen. "Gwen, my dear, you read the letter, what do you make of it? I mean it's clearly from me but why can't the other me do whatever needs doing? Why does the me of here and now need to be there, not that I'm overly concerned, I'm quite looking forward to it really, I must remember to pick up my candle that I left with the girls when I go to Oxford tomorrow, I shall make arrangements to gather the people I need from my letter to myself, I think a little time on the computer is needed tonight for research, right, story time!".

Gwen was left slightly bemused by the fact Merlin had asked a question which she'd been unable to even discuss let alone answer because Merlin had half answered his own question, still, it was all very exciting and she couldn't wait to join him and the boys on another adventure.

"Zoe?" Gwen started, " follow me I think you might be interested in this".

"Oh okay, Harvey! Be a good boy!". Harvey stretched and fell asleep again. Gwen led Zoe upstairs putting her index finger to her lips to signal they should be quiet. They made their way to the boys' bedroom where Gwen slowly pushed their door slightly and both women popped their heads inside to find Merlin sat in an arm chair with Todd asleep on his lap and Noah on the top bunk listening. Noah caught sight of the two women and smiled. Gwen made the silence sign again at Noah to which he smiled and nodded as he watched them both slink back out in to the hallway. They went round to Dave in his study.

"Hello, you two, just been sorting out the spare bed for Merlin and because no doubt he'll be back on the computer half the night, I've booted that up for him too", said Dave.

"I've just introduced Zoe to the unique experience of seeing and hearing Merlin doing bedtime stories" Gwen replied, "first time he did that I was in there too and I fell asleep with Todd, it was magical as you can imagine".

"All very flattering, I'm sure, " came Merlin's voice from behind them, "they do seem to love stories they've not heard before rather than me reading a book or whatever, we continued with the knights of the round table which seems to be extremely popular, Noah assured me their owls will visit later so I was instructed to leave the light on slightly and the two side windows ajar, I hope that's correct?"

"Yes that's fine, " Gwen replied, "We obviously do a quick check later on but the owls are little treasures and do a grand job".

"Definitely worth a check, I've been led to believe the two owls have been getting quite tired lately", Merlin responded. "Are you still ok to drop me off at a bus tomorrow, Dave?"

"Certainly, then just let me know when you're on your way back and I'll come and fetch you, now, how are you doing for modern money? Dave asked".

"Oh don't worry about that, I've plenty, ask me no questions I shall tell you no lies, thank you anyway".

"Ok, Zoe and I will leave you gentlemen to it, anyone want a drink at all?" Gwen offered.

"Not for me, thank you, " was Merlin's reply.

"I'll be down soon, just want to bend Merlin's ear about a few things" Dave said. Gwen and Zoe went down to the kitchen, while Dave turned his attention to Merlin. "So, Merlin," Dave began, "did you get a chance to look through the book I gave you when you were last here? I'm of a mind that really it's a first attempt and should be considered as a draft, so I'd be interested in adding to it greatly, if it's okay and if you can remember I need the names of all of the knights that attended the round table and do you think it would be better to write the book in almost a biographical way from the perspective of one of the knights or indeed King Arthur himself?"

"Okay well, tell you what, bring up on your computer whatever Wikipedia has on the subject and I'll tell you if there's any truth in it and fill in gaps as we go if you like".

"That would be incredible, thank you. And whilst we're in a creative mood, perhaps we can talk more about Kaelyn? Only I have a dash of writer's block with that one," Dave said, turning to the computer, entering his password to unlock the computer from it's sleep and opening an internet browser.

"Yes indeed, I'm fascinated that you should have started writing with that name, as I began to explain before I left for France [1], the name Kaelyn is very well known to me, it's my Mother's name or indeed will be in about 16 years. I'll explain all that when I feel I can, the fact that both you and my Grandmother should come up with the same name is extraordinary and is something I've yet to figure out, but I'm sure it's something simple, sometimes the simplest explanation is the correct one, so we shall see. If I remember correctly from young Noah's synopsis, your Kaelyn is leading a very similar life to my Mother's which in itself is a fascinating coincidence. Fleeing her pursuer through time etc."

The hours went by without much notice, the two men were so focussed on their work that before long, Dave noticed something.

"Merlin, please don't think I'm being rude, I am loving every second of this, but if you look out of the window towards the south, that's daylight! Which means it must be....in fact....yes...it's just gone past 7am we've been working all night, I'm going to suggest a bit of sleep before we get visitors"

"Agreed! Just a few last things to check on the computer if I may, before I turn in".

"Certainly, thank you again for all your input and help with research and your unique and priceless knowledge, Merlin".

"Absolute pleasure! See you in a few hours! Rest well"

"Same to you".

---

[1] This is presumably mentioned in the 3rd book 'Reality Roulette'

Dave left Merlin to his own devices and retired to bed. Gwen opened an eye, "Just be a few hours huh?!"

"Yes, sorry , love, we got a bit involved as you might imagine, we are noting down history, it's such a unique opportunity, Merlin 'is' history, his first hand experience and knowledge is truly astonishing!"

"Indeed, " Gwen replied, "and don't worry I made sure Zoe and Harvey got off okay, she even messaged me to let me know she got home ok, oh and she found Chris and no doubt interrogated him so that's all ok. What time are people arriving tomorrow?"

"I said any time after one should be ok, so, gives us the morning".

"Well it would if we didn't have two excited boys, honestly it's like Christmas with those two if ever family come to visit"

"That's good, night night" Dave said, turning over.

"You mean good morning?" Gwen's retort had fallen on deaf ears, Dave was already asleep.

Chapter Four

Merlin was already awake, downstairs and entertaining the two young brothers. All three of them were enjoying breakfast that they had very competently managed to cobble together between them. Gwen soon joined them giving Dave a precious few more minutes in bed.

"Is it me or is it cold down here this morning?" Gwen remarked out loud.

"Well it is autumn, would you like me to do something about the fire?" Merlin asked.

"Um, yes, I think it's a very good idea, thank you, Merlin".

"No problem at all, nobody get too close to the fireplace, please".

Merlin raised a hand pointed behind him toward the fireplace and a spark appeared from his finger which flew over to the fireplace. Whereupon the fireplace burst into life showing big orange flames reaching up into the shaft leading up to the chimney.

"What a shame Harvey isn't here, he'd love that" remarked Gwen.

"On the contrary, my dear, "Merlin commented, "the last time I did that, he was very unimpressed, in fact it took Will and Bertha a good five or ten minutes to calm him down, poor thing, anyhow, job done, we should all start to thaw out soon".

Noah and Todd were still looking with open mouths at Merlin, then to the fireplace and back to Merlin.

"That was cool!" Todd stated.

"Well technically, it's hot!" Noah said sarcastically.

"Ok you two," Gwen started, "who's going to go and jump on Daddy, he needs to be ready to welcome everyone".

Todd immediately began running towards the stairs.

"We're on it!" shouted Noah as he tried to keep up with his brother. There was a definite thud from upstairs as the two landed on their unsuspecting and no doubt somewhat blurry Father.

"Not overly sure it took both of them, but whatever works", Gwen muttered, "just going to get myself a mug of wake up juice, can I get you anything, Merlin?".

"Not a thing, thank you, I'm full of apple juice and cereal thanks to your wonderful boys".

"Fair enough".

"Anything I can do to help before your imminent invasion?"

"Nope, reckon we're as ready as we're going to be, but Dave will probably find things that need doing".

"I heard that, Morning all!" came Dave's voice from the foot of the stairs, "I'll be right with you all, just going to get something sugary and/or caffeinated in me to try and boot myself up".

"I was just about to do the same thing," said Gwen, "go sit, I'll bring something through".

"Thanks, love. Morning, Merlin, right what's the plan with you today?"

"Morning, Dave. So, I've decided to delay my bus adventure to Oxford until Monday for several reasons. The most important ones being that I promised the boys we'd track future me once it gets dark, far easier that way, plus I'm very keen to include young James in our fun. The other reason being, against my better judgement I found myself looking at bus timetables, seems they operate a very different schedule on a weekend if at all, Sunday being even more restricted and if I ever hope to gain any sense of freedom on their network I feel it's better to pop across after the weekend, if that's agreeable with you?"

"Very sensible, Merlin, I agree, take the weekend to relax, meet some extended family and enjoy time with the boys".

"Fun fact for you, the phrase or reference of 'weekend' or '*the* weekend' simply didn't exist back in my day, it's a reasonably recent term I believe".

"I'll look that up for you, I'd be interested to know too".

"Lovely, what time are we expecting visitors?", Merlin enquired.

"Well interestingly as you may remember I was going to go pick them up from the train station, but a recent message says, it turns out that James' Dad is able to make it after all so they're driving here under their own steam, so I've said any time after one, and being quite punctual as they are gives us a little over three hours I reckon".

"Perfect!"

Sure enough a little over three hours later, a message came through on Dave's phone. it read

---
Almost with you - K x

"Ok!" Dave exclaimed, " Battlestations everyone. Boys, drinks, I'll put the kettle on, Merlin, you sit tight".

By the time Dave had made it out to the kitchen, all instructions had been abandoned and both boys were out the front to welcome the incoming party. Before Dave had a chance to greet people, they were already in. Gwen made no hesitation in making introductions.

"Everyone, this is Merlin, Merlin, this is young James, Noah and Todd's cousin on Dave's side of the family, with his Mum, Kelly and Dad, Ian".

"Charmed", Merlin said, shaking both parents' hands.

"So, you're Merlin are you?" Kelly asked incredulously.

"At your service, young lady", came the reply.

"My side of the family", Gwen stepped in, " always full of little surprises and quirks".

"Lovely to meet you", Kelly offered out of politeness. She had a look of both enchantment and confusion in equal measure.

Gwen leant in and whispered, "I'll explain shortly".

Merlin turned his attention toward young James. "Hello young Sir, tell me, do you like magic?" he asked with a twinkle that seemed to glisten across both eyes at once.

James nodded shyly and managed a "yes, I do" in response.

"Excellent", Merlin continued, "I want you to close your eyes and think of any card from a standard card deck. Once you've thought of it, keep the image of it in your head and focus as hard as you can on it, let me know when you've got it, but don't tell me what it is".

"Okay, got it", said James, his eyes scrunched tightly closed like his hands down by his sides, "not telling you".

"Good lad", Merlin chuckled softly. "Now if you carefully reach in to the top pocket of your shirt".

James did exactly as instructed, he found a playing card in his shirt pocket, pulled it out, to reveal it was the Ace of diamonds.

"Oh!" said James unenthusiastically, "this isn't my card, sorry, I think I know what went wrong though. For some reason, even though I had chosen a card, this exact one kept pushing itself in to my mind, the card literally kept changing in front of me".

"Interesting! Why don't you check your pocket again?" Merlin suggested.

James did so, finding and pulling out a second card and exclaiming "my card!" It was the ace of hearts. "How did you do that?"

"I'm afraid a true magician never reveals his secrets, however I can teach you some magic later, if everyone is in agreement?" Merlin looked at the two Mums and winked.

"Yes please!" announced James, his shyness now left far behind.

"I have just the thing, but we have to wait for nightfall".

Merlin took up residence in the comfy armchair he had sat in before, Before Noah could find the words "hey James, do you want to play upstairs in mine and Todd's room?"Todd and James were already halfway up the stairs, so Noah joined them. Meanwhile, Dave took drink orders from everyone and disappeared into the kitchen to sort them all out, Gwen shouted up the stairs, "boys? Don't forget to drink something please, if you're up there burning energy!"

"Yes Mum / Auntie Gwen!" came the replies. James' Mum pulled up a seat next to Merlin, "Do you mind if I sit here?"

"Oh, please do" Merlin replied. He was unaware curiosity was starting to get the better of her and she had questions.

"So, tell me, Merlin, where do you come from and how do you fit in with everyone here?" was the first line of interrogation. Merlin caught Gwen's eye as she re-entered the room. She smiled and nodded as if to say, "Go for it, I'm here if you need backup".

Merlin took a deep breath and started, "Well, originally I'm from not very far away at all from here really, but I soon moved to Cornwall and have been there for several hundred years". This was the first test to see any reaction, "I married my wife Gwendolyn in the year of our lord 1211, four years later we were blessed with the birth of our daughter, Bertha who will soon be 21! She is currently studying at Oxford university now, I shall try and explain this next part as best I can, if I hadn't witnessed everything unfold before my very own eyes I'm not sure I'd believe it myself". He stopped briefly only to take a large sip of apple juice and catch his breath again. He continued, "Now, where was I? Ah yes, Oxford, now, couple of bits of info for you, Gwen here is my descendent by around 13 or 14 generations we figure, another of my descendents of similar age lives across the county in Marlborough and her brilliant son Will is…dating I believe it's called these days…my daughter, but not to worry, this particular union has been discussed with much interest on several occasions but to take away any complications or concerns, it seems Will was adopted so he's not related in any way so far as we're aware. But here's the kicker, Bertha has made a wonderful new friend with whom she shares a dormitory room with called Katy or Kathryn to give her her full name, however it has since come to light, that young Kathryn is my grandmother, Bertha's great-grandmother, most extraordinary, you really couldn't write it, absolutely incredible".

Gwen stepped forward, "Merlin, sorry to interrupt, but I can tell by Kelly's facial expression that all of this might be a bit too much to take in if you follow me?"

"Ah, yes, quite right, sorry to have filled your head with so much, my dear, I can hardly get my head around it myself, tell you what, let me step away with Dave for a little while, we have much to talk about, regarding family and knights of old, don't we,sir!"

"True, Merlin, join me, no rush, I need to make sure I also dedicate time to being sociable and available to all" Dave responded, meanwhile, Kelly's curiosity was now getting confused but still very much pressing, she turned to Gwen with a concerned look on her face, waiting until Merlin had left the room, she said, "Gwen, I don't mean to appear rude about your guests and obviously this is your house, but where did you find him?"

"Oh, Merlin?" Gwen responded matter-of-factly, "He quite literally appeared in Dave's office upstairs one evening, out of the blue, seems he arrived by candle, another long story, now, I know what you're thinking",

"I'm not a hundred percent you do…"

"Hmmm, well, I don't know how to assure you, but he's absolutely on the level, and he has some unique ways to prove it if you give him a chance, including the whole coming here from Cornwall of 800 years ago bit, his own past family alive and well over in Oxford etcetera, "

"Riiiiiight…" was mostly all Kelly could muster albeit sarcastically..

"Give him time, I guarantee he's eager to prove himself to you, you'll see. Meanwhile, where's your Ian gone?"

"I think he's gone off with Dave and Merlin, probably to try and assess the old man further, Gwen, you don't believe it all do you?"

"I must admit I was hesitant at first, but I've seen things, experienced things, you're going to think I've lost my mind or taken to drink but I swear on my own children's lives that I have been to the past, met his wife, we all did, we were in their house in the 13th century down in Tintagel, I've got photos, I mean look at this, it's their living room in the cave under the castle". Gwen fetched out her phone and showed a photo of what she had just described.

"Oh Gwen, I'm not trying to paint you as a liar but even my non-technical brain knows you can't trust a photo these days, that could be made using that artificial intelligence".

"I swear I'm telling the truth, ask Dave, the boys, I'll introduce you to Zoe if I can, she's Merlin's other descendant over in Marlborough, they visit quite often, she was here only yesterday in fact. Oh and here's a selfie I took with Merlin's wife while we were being held prisoners in Tintagel," Gwen handed her phone over. There was nothing Kelly could say or think, other than it couldn't be real but it was a fantastic story nonetheless. She didn't know what to say or think next. Kelly opted to sit down with her cup of tea and would deal with whatever strange thing happened next. Gwen walked over to put her arms around Kelly and said "I'm so sorry if any or all of this has made you worried or upset, but it was best to tackle it head on, I promise you, Merlin is more harm to himself sometimes than he ever is to anyone else, please try not to judge him or us until we've had chance to prove things, make things a bit clearer and put your mind at rest". Kelly nodded in agreement, smiled and knocked back the rest of her tea.

Chapter Five

A short time later, Dave and Ian returned to the living room. Ian had a large grin on his face. He looked at the two women saying, "I have to say, for all of the crazy sounding stuff Merlin talks about, he's a fascinating man. His knowledge on history is amazing, and as for his ability to turn a normal looking airing cupboard in to a simple yet powerful portal that you can walk in to and emerge somewhere else in the house is brilliant, seriously you need to try it, no idea how it's done, Dave is absolutely insistent that it's all Merlin, there's no trick walls involved".

"Really? A portal in the airing cupboard?" Kelly remarked with an unimpressed and sarcastic tone and facial expression, "whilst you were disappearing in cupboards and popping back out all over the house, did you happen to look in on James?"

"Yes I did, imagine their surprise when I walked straight out of their wardrobe as if I'd been hidden in there the whole time? There was an element of them jumping in there after me, hoping to find Narnia but it seems, according to Merlin, the portal is only one way, apologies, Gwen, only the boys' bedroom, their wardrobe in particular may be a bit of a mess".

"Don't worry, Ian, we're used to it. What, dare I ask, have you done with Merlin? Experience has led me to be curious what he's up to if left to his own devices".

"Never fear, I'm right here everyone, was just shutting the portal down before one of the boys or all of them got trapped in a loop or worse. Now, let's see what I can do for you, young Kelly".

"Why do you need to do something for me?

"Because, it's important for everyone to believe in magic, especially adults, children tend to believe anyway, it's already part of them, I see it as my duty to keep magic and wonder alive". At that point there was a definite rumbling sound coming from…'somewhere' outside,

"Ah, of course!" Merlin muttered. "Dave? I don't suppose we could utilise Henrietta for a group trip to see Dan could we? By my poor excuse for mathematics, there are 8 of us".

"Yes, we can make that happen", Dave answered, "would give the boys chance to get some air and maybe more apples of course, shall I pop upstairs and round them up?"

"Can I ask? Dan? Henrietta?" Kelly directed her line of enquiry at Merlin.

"Back very shortly", Dave announced as he jogged towards the stairs.

"Okay, " Merlin began, " we will need perhaps food, I have everything else required in this very full up brain of mine, to answer your question, young Kelly, Henrietta is the name your cousin Dave has given to one of his fuel driven vehicles which is perfect for visiting 'Dan', short for 'Dandelion' my faithful dragon".

"I'm sorry, your what?"

"Dragon, big, mostly green, breathes fire, you get the idea, the rumbling noise is him snoring up at the cave which is inside the old Ridgeway just south of here, doesn't take long to get there", Merlin described, all quite matter-of-factly. Kelly slowly turned toward Gwen, Gwen was simply nodding back at her as if to say, 'yup,there's a dragon'. James came running into the room closely followed by Noah and Todd and eventually Dave.

"Mummy! Mummy!" James was already out of breath but excitement was keeping his adrenaline in fine form, "Mummy! We're off to see a Dragon!"

"Yes apparently so, I hope this dragon definitely exists otherwise Mr Merlin here is going to be responsible for dealing with a very disappointed young man!"

"Oh, Dan exists!" Todd insisted, "and he's just the beginning, wait until you meet the rest of the animals!"

"Right, " Dave began, "I'll pop out and get Henrietta going, join me when ready everyone!"

The boys could be found jumping up and down in the kitchen, fuelld by mostly excitement with a touch of eagerness and impatience, they wanted to get going! It wasn't long before Dave was at the front door calling for the boys to get them installed before designating seating for the various adults.

"Okay everyone, "Dave began, "welcome aboard Henrietta the All-terrain adventure vehicle, first stop is the apple tree, for the benefit of those who have never been to or heard of this tradition of ours, we will require all available hands for the picking of and putting apples in to the bags which are provided for this very activity and can be found in the boot. From there we will head West to see Dan and the animals. Has everyone used the toilet before we leave?" there was a general murmur of "yes" from everyone in the car including the adults. So Dave headed off in the direction of Chiseldon as they had done countless times before. Everyone fetched a bag and began fetching apples mostly from the ground where they had fallen, Assisted in no small way from when Dan was given free reign over the tree by Merlin on their recent return from France. Ian could be seen stood looking up at the tree. Merlin was the first to approach him saying "you'd be right to think it's better to get the ones nearer the top, however you'd need a long ladder or a dragon for that."

"Oh, hi Merlin, I was just thinking quite randomly of a quote or proverb I've always liked, it goes something like :

'The one who plants trees, knowing that he will never sit in their shade, has at least started to understand the meaning of life.'

"Written by a clever chap from India by the name of Rabindranath Tagore."

"How very interesting that you should think of that, " Merlin commented "it may interest you to know that I planted the seed for this very tree a millenium ago, or at the very least a predecessor. " Merlin smiled and left Ian to continue pondering life and carried on putting apples into a bag. Everyone gathered back at Henrietta, the three boys however had better ideas and were currently climbing up inside the tree, their bags left on the ground so any apples they found on the way up could simply be dropped into them. By the time the adults had followed the sound of the boys shouting at each other, especially Noah who was almost at the top by now, The other two had opted to stay nearer the ground, because as Todd pointed out, even if they got to the top, how would they ever get back down again?

"You okay up there?" Todd shouted up.

"Yes, I'm fine" came Noah's reply, " you'll never guess what I've found!"

"What?" Todd and James both shouted eagerly.

"A lot of the apples up here are red! I'm going to throw some down, so LOOK OUT BELOW!" Noah shouted, He had a decent view of the ground below him so was able to practise some precision bombing, he didn't want to hit anyone, he figured that would hurt from that height, he also factored in the likelihood of being in trouble!

"Hello boys", came Dave's voice, "where's Noah?"

Todd pointed up the tree.

"Ah, ok, you alright up there Noah?" Dave shouted.

"Yes, fine, coming down!" Noah replied.

"Ok, carefully does it"

"Yes, Dad, I know".

After quite a while, Noah hadn't appeared back on the ground.

"Are you sure you're okay?" Dave carefully enquired".

"Well, yes, I'm fine", Noah began to answer, "but, I swear it's all different coming down than when I went up, only, I'm now at a point where there's no available branches to step down on to, is Merlin there?"

"Hello! Did I hear my name?" Merlin shouted up, having just appeared, from around the other side of the tree.

"Merlin, it's me, Noah. I don't think I can get down, it's as though all available branches have moved themselves so I'm kinda stuck!"

"Don't worry, leave it to me, branches do sometimes have a habit of doing just that, rearranging themselves, it's a sort of defence mechanism, the tree re-arranges itself if it thinks it's in danger, quite clever really, let me have a quick word".

"A quick word? With a tree?" Noah asked.

"Certainly!" Merlin answered. "Have you never heard of the 'Wood-Wide Web'? Trees can communicate with each other using a very complex root system all over the world. For me to communicate with this or indeed any other tree via this one, I merely do this". Merlin stepped forward, reached out his hand and placed it on the trunk of the tree. He began to speak quietly and unintelligibly much like he had done with the looking glass beneath Tintagel, obviously magic of some sort, or just good old-fashioned ancient knowledge of which there has been a lot of. Suddenly, because Merlin obviously said the wrong thing or insulted the tree perhaps, he was hit on the head by a large apple from above even where Noah now was.

"Sorry if that was me, Merlin, perhaps I loosened that one while picking them earlier?" Noah tried to apologise through tears of laughter. Seeing a large apple literally bounce off Merlin's head was so funny to see, Noah laughed so hard he nearly fell out the tree.

"Not at all, young man, that was purely my fault, I'm afraid whilst I was once fluent in all tree languages, as the old saying goes, 'use it or lose it' and I've not had an occasion to talk to trees in many years so I think I said the wrong thing, anyway, not giving up". True to his word, Merlin started again and got through the whole thing without being hit on the head again or worse. He then said to Noah, "Ok, if I've got this right, you should see movement and the tree will help you down". Excited and slightly nervous, Noah waited a short while until he saw branches starting to move. Eventually, a large branch made its way just a few feet below where Noah was perched, stopped and shook itself. Noah cautiously lowered himself to the branch but not knowing what was happening next, he decided to sit astride the branch and hang on rather than just stand there. Sure enough, the branch carefully weaved its way around other branches and lowered Noah gently to the ground, whereupon he climbed off, turned to the tree and thanked it.

Todd was the first to come running over to see if Noah was okay, which he was, not a scratch. the adults had been watching the whole event amazed, and had questions, obviously.

"How did you do that, Merlin?" asked Ian.

" I didn't do anything", Merlin replied, "it was clearly all the tree's doing".

"Yes but we saw you talking to it, then after the tree started moving about, it lowered Noah to the ground".

"Yes, it's true, I told the tree that it wasn't in danger and asked would it kindly mind lowering the lad down, if you're polite, generally trees can be quite helpful really, and I have a bit of history with this one, we're old friends really".

"You talked to the tree and it helped Noah down?" Kelly asked incredulously.

"Quite so".

"How does that work then?"

"Well a reliable mix of nature and magic can accomplish most things. Trees are among the oldest and wisest things in nature, this is why it's best to look after them and be kind to them!"

"Hey look at this!" came James' voice as he ran up to his parents. " Noah found red apples while he was up the top of the tree!

"Oh", said Ian, "why would the apples be a different colour at the top? Is that even a possibility?"

"Certainly! As I said before, a mix of nature and magic!" Merlin chuckled with a smile in Kelly's direction.

Meanwhile Noah was being told not to go climbing things including tall trees by his parents.

"Sorry" Noah said to them.

"What if Merlin hadn't been here to ask the tree to help you down?" said Gwen, twitching at the realisation that if what she had just said had been heard by any stranger would sound mad.

" I know, I said sorry, okay?" Noah retorted.

Dave intervened by saying in a loud voice, "right, everyone back to the car". Everyone then made their way back to the car and Dave then set off in a Westerly direction towards Dan's cave.

Chapter Six

Merlin once again suggested he be the first to get out, for obvious reasons, such as being able to communicate with Dan and the others,, even though they were perfectly capable of communicating with humans, Dan in particular was more likely to be more at ease to see Merlin first. Merlin climbed out of Henrietta and made his way to the opening of Dan's cave. He called Dan and was greeted by Mollie the owl who sleepily fluttered out to say "Hello, Merlin and ", looking over to the car " everyone else including some new faces by the looks of it?".

"Hello, Mollie, where's Dandelion?" Merlin asked.

"Oh he's just having a quick nap", Mollie replied, at which point a soft but deep rumble could be heard followed by a tiny puff of smoke flying out of the cave entrance.

"Ah yes, so he is", Merlin remarked, "it's a lovely day, I'm going to suggest we stay around here or nearby until he's had his nap, jolly good idea that, don't disturb him for now, I", Merlin stopped talking when he realised Mollie had flown off to see the boys at the car. Luckily for Mollie, Noah's window was open so she simply, carefully landed herself on his lap, plumped herself up, shook her feathers and settled down ready for a snuggle.

"Oh hello, " Noah said. Todd also carefully offered up a hand to stroke her.

Mollie suddenly had a thought, "hello everyone, Todd, I'll try and get Poem out here, bear with". She pulled herself up to her full height of precisely 1 foot, leaned out of the open window, took a deep breath and screeched with incredible volume. The translation of which was "Poem! Get out here! Todd and Noah are here with some new faces! I mean extra new people,not thst they've literally replaced their own faces, oh for the love of DOG, WAKE UP! Pretend it's dusk, it's not that sunny! Bit cloudy if I'm honest, oh and, BRING A WORM I'M STARVING! POOOOOEM!".

One of the longest two minutes of Todd's life followed but, sure enough, Poem suddenly appeared next to the car and like her sister carefully landed herself, and did the plumping, shaking, settling down thing. After a few minutes, Todd remembered they had James with them.

"James, I'm fairly sure there are no more owls, but I don't mind if you want to borrow mine, she's very friendly and cuddly, doesn't bite, then hopefully soon we can go in and you can meet the other animals. Okay, Poem, I'm going to let you snuggle with James, he is also friendly, cuddly and won't bite. Be nice!". Todd picked up Poem and handed her carefully to James who placed her on his lap, "Thank you, Todd".

"Welcome", Todd responded. He then found himself perfectly placed to be able to stroke both owls at the same time.Merlin popped his head in through Noah's open window to address everyone inside.

Hello all, "he began, "just to keep you all up to date, little Mollie here has informed me that Dandelion is currently taking an afternoon nap, so my suggestion is this. We stay either here or nearby long enough to give the poor thing a good rest. perhaps the owls can bring a few more animals out to meet everyone, if not, no matter, I'm sure we can find something fun to do while we wait a few hours". Everyone seemed to agree.

Dave suddenly announced, "I don't know about anyone else but I feel like a picnic". This got the three boys excited. Dave got everyone to step out the car. James handed Poem back to Todd. Todd and Noah then let them fly back to the cave to see if they could find any other animals that might want to come out and say hello but they were told not to wake up Dan. After clearing the car, Dave opened up the tailgate at the back and with the words "watch this! Everyone stand back", pressed a button which flat-packed all the seating which turned the car into a large area where everyone could sit around facing each other in a sort of circle.

"I spy a flaw in this plan", said Kelly.
"Oh?" Dave enquired.
"Food?"
"Knew I'd forgotten something"

Merlin stepped forward, cleared his throat and continued with, "Ahem, Luckily I considered this very issue back at the house, now, if you'll allow me, I took the liberty of gathering everything we could need or want, I'll need some help with this".

"You brought a picnic with you?" Kelly asked.

"Yes sort of, well I figured we'd all want to eat at some point and there's not really anywhere around here we can simply get any food or drink for that matter".

"So, how's this going to work? There's nothing in the car".

"Well, if Dave and Ian are feeling strong if they'd care to follow me for a moment?"

"Certainly" both men answered simultaneously. Merlin beckoned them towards some trees just a few hundred yards away. He needed somewhere out of the way. The three men reached a small clearing just inside the clump of trees at which point Merlin stopped.

"Now, imagine if you will, "he began, "if like me you are vaguely familiar with the concept of cloud storage for computer data? Well, I've created the same sort of thing but with physical objects, so, I've stored what I've prepared for today in a sort of virtual pantry which I shall now summon or in modern terms 'log-in' to, to gain access then we simply open it up and pull the stuff out. I'm being basic of course it's more complicated than I'm making it sound but I think the analogy is a good one, so, in your words, Dave, 'stand back' and I shall summon the pantry".

Some unintelligible words and most-likely overly-dramatic arm and hand gestures later, there was a flash of flight and suddenly there was a door in front of them. Merlin simply stepped forward, opened the door and said, "Okay gentlemen, if you would kindly step in here you will hopefully find a large wicker basket if you could retrieve it and carry it back to the car. Hopefully it won't be too heavy for you both, If it is obviously I have a solution for that too, ignore all the other stuff in there, I'll explain some of that another time".

Dave and Ian both looked at each other for a brief moment and almost like they were linked psychically, they walked toward the open door, stepped inside and were unsurprised to find a large wicker basket as promised just inside a vast room which looked like the tomb of an Egyptian monarch, full of treasures and various artefacts.

"Can't wait to hear all about his explanation for all this!" said Dave.

"Indeed!" Ian agreed.

The two men lifted the somewhat heavy basket back out the door to find Merlin was nowhere to be seen so they made their way back to the car. They asked the surprised group back at the car if they'd seen Merlin. Todd pointed and announced "he's stood right there, next to you, Daddy". He was absolutely right, everyone could see him. Even Dave and Ian could see him standing there. They put down the hamper and turned to Merlin.

"Where did you come from?" asked Dave, "When we came out with this basket as asked, you were nowhere to be found".

"Apologies, gentlemen, I needed to pop in to the pantry myself to check on something, but I was with you all the way back here, making sure you were okay, didn't mean to concern you".

"Pantry?" Kelly and Gwen both asked simultaneously.

It's a full storage room hidden just over there in those trees. I'll try and explain later".

"Riiiiight, okay", was Kelly's response. Gwen simply shrugged as if to suggest that nothing really surprised her anymore. The large picnic basket/hamper thing was lifted into the back of Henrietta, and everyone was encouraged to climb in and find space to sit with the hamper in the middle.

"Right everyone, the way this works is, everything you would want is inside, just search for what you're after" Merlin explained.

"Oh come on, how can that possibly work?" Kelly exclaimed, "I'm doing my best to accept talking owls, portals from one cupboard door to another and random pantries in the countryside but, I draw the line at being able to reach inside this basket and pulling out this large punnet of fresh strawberries!" It suddenly dawned on her that a large punnet of strawberries was now sat in front of her. "Oh!" she opened the box, "Yup, those are definitely fresh, wonderful strawberries, who wants to try some?" All three boys clambered over saying "yes please" while grabbing a strawberry each. They all agreed they were really good strawberries.

"I know what this needs!" Noah declared. He moved to the hamper, opened the lid, reached in and pulled out a large pot of fresh cream. "This!" His idea was met with approval from everyone, by now everyone had tried a strawberry and was very impressed by it. Meanwhile Merlin had just produced a strawberry ice lolly from his left sleeve. He caught James witnessing this and said "I'm very partial to these ever since I discovered them recently". James looked longingly at it, Merlin saw this too and looked from James to the hamper and back again as if to say 'you know what to do, look inside'. Sure enough James also found a strawberry ice lolly inside.

"Well I must say, Merlin", Kelly started, "this is all very impressive!"

"Thank you, my dear, coming from you I take that as a very great compliment".

"I'm sorry I was so sceptical, I must admit I'm still a bit unsure about everything but, I'm loving your work" Kelly laughed.

"Nothing wrong with scepticism, it's simply your way of ensuring you're not taken for a fool. I promise you I only ever use magic or a hopefully good impression of it, for good, never bad".

"Excuse me" came a voice from the back door of the car.

"It's Barry!" said Todd, "James, he's a badger!"

"Yes I can see that, wow!" James replied.

"Hello my dear fellow", said Merlin, "how are you?"

"Great thanks," Barry replied, "just to let you know, most of us are starting to stir, the owls let us know you're here, Dan is also starting to wake up"

"Wonderful I shall pop in very soon"

"Good good, and who are the new faces I see here?" Barry was introduced to everyone and they to them.

"We've got an Uncle Barry, haven't we Mum" James declared.

"Just to save confusion, James' Uncle Barry and our Grandad Barry are the same person" Noah said.

"Ah ok, I understand, I think" Barry answered, "I'll see you all inside I hope, I'm going to pop back in as I can see the sun is starting to set, bye for now".

Everyone waved the badger goodbye, Merlin told everyone he was also going to quickly pop in to the cave so as not to startle Dan with everyone appearing at once, though at that precise moment a deep rumble was both felt and heard "Master?"

Merlin climbed out of the car and made his way to the cave entrance, "Hello Dan, on my way" Merlin announced. Everyone else was told to remain in the car until fetched by, probably, Merlin.

A terrific feast continued full of everyone's favourite picnic food, it was agreed they should definitely do this more often.

"I tell you something I've not had in an absolute age", said Gwen, "I wonder, First thing first before we get too excited, aha, perfect!" she reached in the box and pulled out a pack of plastic tumblers which would work perfectly as drinking glasses. "Right next up, I would like….a…" she reached in the hamper again, to pull out a "large bottle of dandelion and burdock! Absolutely amazing, boys, I used to have this a lot at your ages, it's quite an old fashioned drink but my Nan used to create her own, wonderful". Gwen poured the drinks out for everyone. The boys seemed reasonably impressed by it, which was the big test out of the way and the grown-ups relished in their own levels of nostalgia with the drink, which they had all tried at least once in their childhood.

Chapter Seven

Meanwhile in Dan's cave, Merlin was trying to convince Dan of another potential journey explaining about the letter he had received from himself and young Todd's theory about the letter coming from the North pole. Dan was not sure about a trip to somewhere so cold, the south of France was lovely because of the warmth.

"Not to worry, you do know I'll never let you get cold, "Merlin assured his enormous pet, "oooh, talking of which, is it me or is time getting away from us? If I'm not mistaken it'll begin to get dark outside soon". Merlin was peering longingly into the sky through a sort of window in the cave wall. A very small window though, and no glass, just a small opening letting in a little air, just big enough to fit a small owl through. "I'll be right back, just going to check on the others" Merlin announced as he made his way to the exit of the cave. He made his way across the large space outside to find everyone still sat patiently in Henrietta, he popped his head round the corner of the open tailgate at the back, just as Barry the badger had done earlier. He greeted everyone with a resounding and cheerful "hello all! I hope you're all okay out here, I apologise for being so long, time quite literally got away from me. quick question. Mostly for Dave, I have a need to pop up to Barbury castle, up on the old ridgeway, could I persuade you to drive me up there? And would you all be ok with that?" There was a general sound of agreement from everyone, especially the three boys though, they all agreed they weren't sure why they were excited by the idea, perhaps just the idea of another adventure with Merlin, the word castle probably helped. Of course, Noah and Todd had been on previous Merlin adventures but James didn't know what to expect. Dave was in agreement, so much so he fired Henrietta up straight away without really thinking about it. "I'll take that as a yes then, " Merlin remarked, "many thanks, I shall just let the animals know then I'm all yours".

"Right, " said Dave, "everyone out, I'll put the seats back as they were, I suggest putting the hamper in the boot for now". Everyone jumped out of the car, in some cases literally. Dave made his way round to the back of the car, he and Ian lifted the hamper into the boot which thankfully did fit, though presumably if needs be it could go back in Merlin's magic pantry in the trees, but it was a great thing to keep with them if they could. Dave pressed the button that had previously flattened all the seating and all the seating reset itself to the original configuration, "now that's 'my' attempt at magic, do love that feature, everyone in!" Everyone climbed aboard yet again. Gwen spotted Merlin approaching.

"Merlin, do you want to sit up front for 'giving directions' purposes? I can jump in the back with Kelly, Ian and the boys".

"Oh, only if you're sure my dear, I don't mind giving instruction from the back".

"No no, you hop in the front, I insist" said Gwen, grinning.

Merlin did as he was told and wasted no time in getting comfortable up front.

"So, Barbury castle is it, Merlin? What's the plan this time? Bit of sunset watching?" asked Dave.

"Well actually, you're nearer the truth than you realise," Merlin replied, "I need a high vantage point and Barbury will be perfect, why do you think the Romans chose it? Clever lot those Romans ya know? Do you need directions?"

"No no, we regularly visit Barbury as a family, it's quite the attraction for people who like to walk, take in nature, try and connect with the local past, that sort of thing".

"How extraordinary. Before we set off, " Merlin did his best to turn himself where he could communicate with everyone in the back. " Todd, could I ask you a favour?"

"Yes, of course" came the reply.

"Would you reach into the hamper and retrieve one of your rainbow cookies? I'm rather partial to them".

"Do you mean the ones I invented that go with the rainbow hot chocolate?"

"That's them!"

"Oh ok, " Todd then clambered over everyone to get to the back, managed to lift the lid of the hamper slightly, reach in and pulled out a rainbow themed paper bag. He then clambered back to his seat nearer the front, he opened the bag which had several cookies inside, the smell from which was nothing short of mouth-wateringly incredible. Todd leaned forward from his seat and offered up the open bag in Merlin's direction.

"Thank you, young man. I have to say I've found myself almost hallucinating about these, they really are very satisfying and extremely tasty."

Todd offered the bag around at which point he had a question. "Merlin?"

"Yes, lad?"

"A question!"

"Ooooh, exciting!"

"How did you know about my rainbow cookies? I don't remember telling you about them"

"Oh I have my ways, it's a secret even to me sometimes, I don't remember when or where I discovered them but I've been a big fan since, you should make a recipe book of all your ideas, your Dad could help you create it, I think it would do well."

"Yup!" was the noise that came out of Dave as he could be seen visibly nodding and focusing on his rear view mirror while he reversed Henrietta to make her face in a different direction.

"Todd" said Noah with a mouth ready to burst from too much cookie, however, he managed to say the following, "one word, yum!".

Todd managed a "thanks" in return which didn't really put across the inner glow he felt that his big brother approved of his creation.

Dave checked everyone was ready and indeed all strapped in with seatbelts and headed up and over Dan's cave where he then headed slightly NorthWest. The journey was short as their destination was not far away. In fact there were still cookies ,this is an important fact worth noting. Dave made his way to a car park that he would usually park at and pulled up in the 2nd car park which was usually more empty than the first that had toilets and refreshments. They were facing North and could see across the direction of the Cotswolds.

"Brilliant work, Dave, many thanks, won't be a moment, just need to check something". Merlin then stepped out of the car and went to stand on a grass bank in front of the car. After just a few minutes he returned to the car, "As suspected we are not long from sunset, and early evening. Perfect, if I could ask one last favour"?

"Certainly".

"We should return to the cave. Please"

"Righto, everyone get comfortable and buckle up and could I also have a cookie please?"

Dave started the car, retrieved a cookie from the bag that was being dangled next to him. After a short while Dave was parking up next to the entrance of Dan's cave, there was a loud bang and a rumbling sound to accompany it. A large cloud of black smoke puffed out of the cave.

"What was that?" James asked.

"Dan burped" answered Todd.

"Dragons can burp?"

"Well, this one can, and does!"

James found this funnier than almost anything ever. His giggling started Todd giggling too which just started an uncontrollable gigglefest between the two boys, Noah tried his absolute hardest to rise above it all, but found himself starting to laugh with them. Once the giggling started to get a bit quieter, Merlin turned to talk to the boys again.

"Now", he began, "there is something I want to show you boys later, or at least get you to join in with", this got Noah and Todd's attention because they both knew Merlin was probably talking about the tracking thing he wanted to do, James didn't know anything about that yet, plus which he was still playing an animation of a burping dragon in his mind which he was finding very difficult to stop because it was just so funny. Merlin continued, "now the thing I want to do requires us to wait until it gets dark which should happen in just two more hours by my estimate. So the things we need to think about in the meantime, is making sure people are fed and watered, well, we have the hamper for that, we all need to keep warm, I have a few ideas for that but the most obvious one is to keep Henrietta warmed up so we can get heat from her, certainly saves having to set fire to something, plus which she's nice and dry though I am rather hoping for a clear night, do any of you happen to know the weather forecast for tonight?"

"I can keep Henrietta running, but it's a fairly uneconomic way of doing things also it's not overly brilliant for the environment, just my quid's worth of opinions thrown into the pot for consideration" was Dave's comment on Merlin's ideas.

"Understood, Tell me, does Henrietta have an awning of sorts?" Merlin asked.

"No, sorry, never really needed one" Dave answered.

"Not to worry. Right, everyone, including the young boys, please follow me outside for a moment" Merlin announced. He stood by the side of the car and waited for everyone to assemble, which they eventually did. "Right please follow me but all stick together please, no wandering off!"

Chapter Eight

The group followed Merlin who led them over to the clump of trees he had taken Dave and Ian into earlier to fetch the hamper, he stopped when he reached a door stood by itself in the clearing inside the trees. Meanwhile back in Dan's cave, Mollie the owl was trying to get her sister Poem's attention. "Poem, exciting news!".

"Ooooh, what is it?"

"Merlin has just gone into some trees across the way, you know what that means don't you?"

"The pantry!" Poem said with wide eyes. "I've wanted to be nosey in there for a very long time".

"Exactly, let's go"

"He won't let us in, Mollie"

"He might"

"Never has before"

"Won't know if we don't try"

"True".

With that the two owls flew out of the cave and towards the trees.
Merlin was still stood in front of the pantry door facing the others.

"Right okay all, please don't get in the way of the door, once opened, you may all enter. You may look around at everything, go anywhere, ask questions, boys, feel free to touch anything in the 'games room' . I've done my best to label everywhere and everything properly so you shouldn't get lost or too confused. And remember nobody will ever be more than one room away from anywhere or anyone else no matter how far you go, so if you need me just shout, Oh and Poem and Mollie, yes you may come in too. Don't think I don't know you're up there in the tree". The owls looked at each other, slightly stunned that they had been found out. They both fluttered down and got comfortable in Noah's and Todd's hoods they had on their jackets. Merlin made no delay in getting the large pantry door open, everyone walked in to find themselves in a large long hall. There were more doors on both sides and above each door was a large plaque with the name of the room.

James was the first to find a room called "Games room" He instantly shouted out "Noah! Todd! Games!" and was still pointing with his arm out pointing to the sign above the door when Noah and Todd came running up to join him. The three boys instinctively ran to the door at the same time and all pushed it open together. They were presented with a large screen just inside the door. It read "Welcome to the games room, first choose how many of you are playing, this screen uses touchscreen technology so either choose a number from the numbers below or use the on-screen keyboard to type a number". Noah seemed the obvious person to do this as he was the tallest and could reach the top of the screen if needed, so he took it upon himself to step forward and press the number three. From here a voice was heard, "welcome three players, what are your names? You can speak instead of typing, I will hear and understand you". Assuming he was now the designated person in charge, Todd and James both looked at Noah which he took as the hint to step forward. "Hello, my name is Noah", Todd stepped forward saying, "I'm Todd", James was then last to introduce himself.

"Welcome, " the voice continued, "Noah, Todd and James, any game you can think of is available to you including board games, card games, computer games and many more, the choice is unlimited, now all you have to decide is will you all be playing together or individually? You can always change your mind by calling me, you simply say 'Computer' to call me and I can answer your questions". The boys looked at eachother, none of which was sure where to start. The computer voice came back again, "Hello again, " it said, "I have been listening in to your conversations and I can help you if you wish?"

The boys looked at eachother and all nodded in agreement. Before Noah had a chance to respond, the computer voice said "Very well. One of you wishes to have access to all the latest handheld console games with some sort of internet access for streaming and multiplayer functionality, another one of you is very keen on puzzle games, and to really mix things up another has expressed interest if only slightly sub-consciously in the idea of being able to play with a large group of friends. I can make any or all of this happen and can change it entirely for each of you individually or as a group or team as often as you wish. My suggestion is to put you all in a gaming arcade which includes things such as a large computer arcade, bowling alley, a board game cafe and much more, it would contain all these things and whatever you can dream up all in one premises meaning you can all find each other easily if you wish to go off and do your own thing. You'll be armed with hi-tech walkie-talkies for summoning one another and you can do the same with friends you meet and make along the way like team mates in big games, that way you have variety and the ability to each choose along the way. Saying the command "Computer, exit!" will bring you straight back here so you never have to worry about losing anyone or indeed each other". This all sounded amazing.

"Computer, question!" Noah said loudly.

"Yes, Noah, fire away" the computer voice answered.

"Well, How did you figure all of this out? Only a lot of things you mentioned weren't mentioned when we were talking to ourselves".

"I have very good hearing, even if you didn't actually say something, you might have been thinking it, and I'm also very well educated in deciphering body language and I'm constantly scanning you so I can tell your mood, I am also a very advanced lie detector, so be very careful what you think about and wish for. If you look on the floor you will see little lights which make a path, please follow this path until you come to a door. When you're ready, push open the door and enter either together or individually and remember, just say 'Computer' if you ever need me". Todd and James were already 50 yards ahead of Noah and running away, following the lights very quickly. Noah took a nonchalant attitude, taking his time to follow the other two. As the lit path took Noah round a corner he was just in time to see Todd and James disappear through a door. Curiosity got the better of him so he decided to open the very same door which led him into a sort of log cabin. There were windows through which Noah could see a large snowy landscape. On the walls were jackets under which were boots, all of which were fur-lined. In the roof were many sledges of different bright colours. There was also a sort of shelving on one wall which held goggles and woolly hats. Todd and James could be seen changing into what had now become obviously winter gear.

"Hi Noah, " said James, "glad you've joined us, I think this is all my fault, I was imagining sledging and snowball fights, and we found this place. I think we're supposed to get changed into this stuff, so we are".

Noah had no argument, so he joined them in getting changed ready for presumably snow games. There were a few voices that could be heard, gradually getting nearer. A door at the other end of the cabin opened and two children popped into the room. They were dressed like children from the 19th century, probably because that's exactly where they were from. They stepped forward, and the boy of the two strangers spoke.

"Hello, sorry to startle you, let me introduce ourselves. I'm Tim, and this is my sister, Lucy". Lucy stepped forward, " Hello, I'm Lucy, nice to meet you all, you're new, where did you come from?"

"Hi, I'm Noah, and this is my brother Todd and our cousin James, you're new to us too, where are you both from?"

"Originally, we're from London, England ", said Tim, "but now we live in the Rainbow Quarter, you'll be able to see it if and when you step outside. It's best to wrap up warm though, it's jolly cold outside!"

"Yes, looks it, good advice!" said Todd, who wasn't sure why but couldn't take his eyes off Lucy, she was very pretty, wavy blonde hair and big blue eyes, she was staring at Todd too.

"This might sound like an odd question, "Lucy began, aiming her questioning in Todd's direction, "I do hope you don't mind my asking,but do you happen to have a relation such as a sister or perhaps a cousin here in the Rainbow Quarter? Only you resemble a friend of ours very much".

"Sorry to interrupt and, sorry Todd I'm not stopping you from answering, but I must know, what is the Rainbow Quarter? As far as we knew we were in the Games Room inside Merlin's magic pantry. We originally come from a town called Swindon in Wiltshire"

"And I come from quite near London where you're from!" James threw into the conversation.

"Oh, "Lucy replied, "our friend, who's name is Summer, who Todd and Noah resemble greatly, isn't sure where she comes from originally, I've never heard of Swindon I'm afraid. To answer Noah's question, the Rainbow Quarter, oh how do I word this? It's a place for the lost souls of children, children who never got to be born or for whatever reason were given up for adoption or didn't live long enough to reach adulthood, or even sometimes, children who one day just didn't know who they were or understand where they belonged. It's a wonderful place and there are many of us, we all have our own rooms and access to things like the games room here, where we can all play together or by ourselves, it's truly magical. The whole thing was made possible by Father Christmas who has his magic home just over the next mountain, beyond the magic forest".

"Father Christmas?" asked Todd, "you mean he's actually here?"

"Oh yes, "Tim replied, "he and his wife are like parents to all of us, it's such a blessing, if you'll let us, we can show you around, I'm sure it would be allowed, so many of us have arrived here because of different circumstances, everyone is welcome, you are all still children I'm guessing?"

"Oh yes, we're not adults, " Noah replied, "I'm twelve, Todd is eight…"

"Oh Lucy's eight aren't you!" Tim announced.

"Yes that's right, "Lucy agreed, at which point Todd and Lucy smiled at each other. "I'm seven, " said Tim

"And I'm eleven, "said James.

"So, just a small thing, " Noah started to question, beginning to come to his senses, "how come you're in our games room? Computer? Are Tim and Lucy a simulation as part of James' game? A hologram perhaps?"

Tim and Lucy looked confused because of words Noah was using which they didn't understand. Imagine their surprise when the computer answered, "No, Noah, Tim and Lucy are both perfectly real but have access to their own version of the games room, which has been installed in the Rainbow Quarter and linked to this games room. It is just coincidence that Tim and Lucy's request matched James' so closely that the parts from both rooms connected so you are all sharing the same game environment but from different locations. The games room in the Rainbow Quarter was also installed by Merlin just like this one, you'd best ask him about that though".

"Excuse me for asking, "Tim now had a question, "you've now mentioned a Merlin more than once…"

"I've got this one, "Todd answered, "So yes, we are talking about '*the*' Merlin, as in the mediaeval wizard of legend.

"Right, okay, because, "Tim replied, "presumably we're talking about the same gentleman, pointy hat, long beard, does incredible magic, we've met him too, he helped install the games room, so it makes sense that your games room and ours are linked, they must be pretty much the same thing?"

There were general murmurs of agreement from everyone. Noah then announced , "I think it's probably a good idea that we return to 'our' Merlin and let him and our parents know that not only are we okay but try and convince them of what has happened here".

"Good idea!" James agreed,

"I've had an idea, " Todd chipped in, he looked at Lucy and continued, "if we all want to meet again, we ought to agree on a game environment, even if it's this again, Tim and Lucy, were you both given walkie talkies like us? These things", Todd held up his walkie talkie, "we haven't tried them yet but apparently we can all talk to each other using them.

"That is correct, " came the computer's voice again, " you simply press and hold the button on the side and anyone with another walkie talkie can hear you, but don't forget to let go of the button to allow others to reply, and don't forget you can locate anyone within the games room by saying 'Computer locate, followed by the name of the person you're trying to find'.

Before going their separate ways, the five children hugged as a group and said goodbye. Noah, Todd and James left by the door they had entered by. Tim and Lucy did the same. While standing on the lit path outside the door, Noah suddenly remembered something, "We're going about this all wrong!" He then said, "okay you two both repeat after me - Computer! Exit!" Noah vanished instantly which was a bit of a shock, but Todd and James both repeated Noah's instruction, and all three were suddenly stood outside the door marked 'Games room' in the large hall of doors. Now they had to locate the adults. James remembered what Merlin had said about never being more than a room away from anyone. So they could either go opening doors or call out. They chose both. Todd and James were the loudest so they started shouting out names while Noah wanted to see if he could see a door name which would make sense to find people in. Meanwhile Tim and Lucy had made their way back to their own rooms inside the Rainbow quarter dormitories and agreed to meet up later for supper. They had both acquired watches recently so agreed on 6pm. Noah had found a room with the label 'Dad Cave', this had to be his Dad's choice if he'd found it himself, he found himself knocking first before trying to open the large door. Dave's voice could be heard from the other side of the door, "come in?" he sounded surprised. Who on earth would be knocking on this door? Noah turned the handle and entered the room.

"Oh, hello Noah, you okay?"

"Yes thanks, you won't believe what has been happening with Todd James and me, we've met other children from a different place altogether, I think at one point we were in the North pole! Lots of snow, a brief mention of Father Christmas, all a bit of a giveaway, anyway where's everyone else?"

"I'm not sure, lost your Mother hours ago, think she found a shopping mall, Merlin as ever, could be anywhere at any time, you know how he is, come and look at this", Dave led the way through a door which led in to a kind of workshop full of tools, an old radio in the corner was playing music from the 1980s.

"This is very you, Dad, even the music is old".

"Hey, it's not that old, I remember this music when it was new and I'm not old"

"You are a bit, sorry".

"Cheek! Right here's what I want to show you, over here is something under a large tarpaulin". Dave pulled at the tarpaulin until it slid off to reveal an old car that it was covering. Noah's mouth fell open at the sight. "What you are looking at here, is a car that Grandad Barry had when I was your age, maybe a bit younger. It's a 1967 Ford Corsair, the colour is called midnight blue, he did have a light blue one too, but this was the best one in my opinion. It seems I can have anything in this 'Dad cave' so I thought a garage of sorts with a workshop attached would be perfect. At some point I need to get Grandad in here, he'd love it".

"Are we able to get in the car to look?" Noah asked eagerly.

"Yes of course, there's a button next to the handle that you press to open the door, I'll pop round the other side, see you inside".

They both climbed inside the old car. Dave turned on the original radio which was still tuned to a radio station which was playing music of the time the car was originally built, so late 60s. Perfect. After telling Noah all about the different features of the car they decided to climb out and go look for the others.

"Are you going to want to get any other cars in here, Dad?"

"I like American cars from the 50s, so a cadillac would be great, an original Ford thunderbird which is not hugely dissimilar to the corsair, you can kind of see the evolution from one to the other, but, when I was 17 or so years old I had an old Mark 3 Cortina, I'd love to see one of those again, I'll try and find a picture of it for you, right, let's see where everyone got to", they made their way out of the original door to the 'Dad cave' and back out to the hall of doors.

"Right, I left your Mother going in to a door up this way", said Dave starting to walk back up the hall towards what would logically be where they all first entered. Noah followed. They stopped at a door which looked different to the others. It was more plastic looking. Pale blue with a large yellow bar across it for a handle. And sort of screwed to the door was a metal plate which had the words 'This way to the high street'.

"Yup, this is the one, " Dave said. However before they had a chance to open the door, it swung open and they were greeted by Gwen and Kelly who had obviously had a great time.

"Hello gentlemen", said Gwen, "you found each other then? Where are Todd and James?"

"Oh I left them back by the games room way down there", said Noah pointing, " I expect they went back in, it's awesome!"

"Anyone seen or heard from Ian?" asked Kelly

"I'm right here!" came Ian's voice as he approached them from somewhere else, "It turns out that this place becomes something of a museum if it's something you desire and Merlin is the perfect person to walk around a museum with, he has incredible knowledge of most things and was there when most of the displays were in their original place of origin or indeed where it was discovered, though his knowledge of dinosaurs was a bit sketchy so I helped fill in some holes there, seems because they weren't really discovered until the mid 19th century he hadn't really encountered them either when they were alive or later when they were discovered, documented and shown to the world. If you'd said just yesterday pr at any time I would be helping to educate Merlin I wouldn't have believed it. I seem to have lost him again now though. How have you all been getting on?"

"I've been reliving my past with an old classic car" said Dave.

"I was playing with other children we found in a place called the rainbow quarter, then found Dad with this cool old car", was Noah's contribution.

"Kelly and I discovered that this door allows you to go into a high street of sorts or shopping mall that is full of all the shops you could ever want or need, even nostalgic ones, Kelly and I just lost a few hours in an old branch of Woolworths!"

"Ah, Woolies! Classic!" Dave said, reminiscing.

Noah wasn't really sure what the grown-ups were talking about but figured he could bring it up in conversation again another time, if he didn't remember it obviously wasn't important enough to him.

Chapter Nine

"If everyone follows me we can find Todd and James, probably by or in the 'games room'", Noah announced.

And so he started to walk back down the large hall and everyone else followed. Todd and James were in fact, sat on a stone bench opposite the door to the 'games room' with a Merlin between them. The two boys had spent their time telling Merlin everything that had happened, including meeting Tim and Lucy. So by the time everyone else walked up to them, Merlin was more or less up to date on everything to do with the adventure that happened inside the 'games room'. Noah filled in a few more details, specifically about the other 'games room' inside a place called the Rainbow quarter, and the fact Father Christmas had been mentioned and that Tim and Lucy said they had met Merlin too, and that he was apparently the one that installed their version of a 'games room'.

"Extraordinary!" Merlin exclaimed. Absolutely extraordinary that you should find your way to the North pole in that way, right if you could all follow me, there is one more thing I need to do and show you while we're here. We shall take a short cut!". Merlin stood up and made his way to an adjacent hallway, where he and those following made their way past even more doors of many different sizes, colours and materials.After a few minutes, they reached a very modestly smaller door which simply said 'All other routes' on it. He opened it and walked through it into a much smaller hallway. At the far end of this smaller hall was a spiral staircase leading up. It led down too, somewhere, but it was up that was the most important direction for Merlin's purpose. Despite the staircase disappearing out of sight, they all reached the top remarkably quickly. Directly opposite was a door made entirely of stained glass with a picture of stars, planets and other cosmic imagery. Above it was a sign which read 'Observatory'.

"Okay everyone", Merlin began, "as you can see from the sign above the door, this is the observatory. Inside this door is a very powerful telescope and a few other rare and precious artefacts, Ian these should interest you in particular, it's part of the ongoing construction of the museum section of all this, so please everyone, be that bit more careful in here, there are things in here that not even I can replace, I thank you in advance for your care and respect for the things you are about to see, right bear with me for just a moment". Merlin turned to the door, quietly said some presumably magic words and the door could be heard unlocking itself and then opened fully.

Merlin entered the observatory, leaving everyone behind outside the door. A few moments later, he popped his head back out the door, "Well? Aren't you coming in? Time and tide and all that, if we don't shake a leg, we'll miss it!".

Chapter Ten

"Miss what"? Todd asked out loud without realising.

"Well", Merlin continued, "So, this is the whole reason I brought you here, Noah and Todd, you've both joined me on magical adventures, but young James here needed to experience it first hand, as did his Mum and Dad, so here's the next part. As previously mentioned back at the house in Swindon, I wanted to do some tracking, but I needed the right equipment, the right time, the right location and this would be perfect I thought, because there were plenty of things to keep you all entertained while I was waiting. So, allow me to demonstrate how this enormous telescope works. Much like a regular one really, this is the eyepiece for you to look through and over here under this dust cover is a monitor of sorts so, because only one person can look through the telescope at a time, the monitor will allow the rest of you to see what the viewer can see. So, what would we like to see first?"

"Saturn please!" James requested.

"After that", Todd spoke up, "can we see if there are any bad guys on the moon? Like aliens, I know perhaps we should look at Mars for aliens, but if they're on the moon, we know we need to act quicker!"

"Todd, you're weird, but I love you anyway, "said Noah, "Merlin, what would you recommend? Is there anything that NASA haven't found yet? Like planets we don't know about? In our solar system I mean".

"Okay boys let's do this in order", Merlin began, "First up is Saturn, let me get it right for you, young James, now, let's see what we can find". Merlin began turning various wheels and controls while looking through the main eye-piece. "That's annoying, bit of cloud cover this evening, but no matter, I have a solution for that", Merlin cast a bit more magic which scattered the cloud away and gave a much clearer view of the night sky, "that's better, you're in luck, young man, Saturn is in an excellent position right at this moment, step up here and take a look. I'll switch on the monitor for everyone else". James stepped up onto a wooden platform making him tall enough to see through the actual eye-piece of the colossal telescope. Meanwhile, Merlin was getting frustrated with the monitor, occasionally hitting the back of it to see if that would make a difference, sure enough after a few minutes a picture started to appear.

"Wow!" James gasped, "Look how clear it is! Look at those rings, they're amazing". Todd started to think about onion rings and was getting impatient for his turn at the telescope. Finally, James had seen enough for now but was keen to have another go later if allowed.
"Okay, Todd, first up, the moon, have a look at that", said Merlin, adjusting the platform for Todd to stand on. Todd looked through the eye-piece and could see the moon in very clear detail.
"What can you see, Todd?" Noah asked.
"Not a lot, look at the monitor! No aliens, no bad guys, so that's good!" Todd answered.
"Stay as you are Todd, I'm just going to adjust the telescope so you can look at Mars, as requested".
Mars suddenly came into view. Merlin took Todd's right hand and placed it on a control on the side of where he was looking with the instruction "use this to zoom in and out, might help you to get a bit closer to things".
"Thanks Merlin. Not seeing much here either, mostly rock, anyone else?"
There was nothing to see as Merlin expected. Todd was desperately trying to get more time on the telescope, but Merlin lightly tapped him on the shoulder, "sorry, I need the telescope back again, I promise you can have another go later, you all can in fact, but for now, there is something that I must do, and for this part I shall need Noah because it fulfils his request too! Noah if you could step up here, I'll lower the platform a little for you as you're that bit taller. Now, let's see, I took the liberty of finding stars which act like mirrors. Why you ask? Well, I need to use the theory that what we are looking at takes an amount of time to reach our eyes given it's distance from us if it were travelling to us at the speed of light. So for instance, if we look at something that is one light year away, that means, the image has

travelled to us at the speed of light and has taken one year to reach us at that speed. Now here's a theory for you, if someone stood on a planet 200 million light years away and if they had a telescope powerful enough to see the earth from that distance, they could see dinosaurs roaming around. I'm not explaining myself very well, but basically we are always looking into the past, the further we can see, the further back in time we can see. Now, what if we were able to refine that, by having relays? By which I mean, something that would divert our vision in a different direction, break down the distance? So, I have discovered that stars work as magnificent mirrors which allow us to tweak our direction of travel and slow down the speed at which our sight reaches a given destination, meaning we can look anywhere at any time. At least, that's the theory, so, I have a time and place in mind. For this, I need coordinates, in this case, geographical coordinates, I was always better with time rather than location, but this is a no-brainer, okay, bear with me everyone while I tap in the numbers on this terminal. Noah, don't get too close to the telescope's eye-piece for a moment, it will start to move shortly". Merlin began feeding the telescope's control panel with data, as predicted the telescope started moving but not before a lot of mechanical whirring. This went on for a good five minutes, after which Merlin addressed the assembled throng.

"Okay everyone, if you would care to turn your attention to the monitor, Noah, you can now look into the eye-piece directly, now, I shall also check the monitor, ah yes, right, what you can all hopefully see here, is the North Pole, the Northernmost point of our home planet, the time is now, not in the past, just getting my bearings you see".

The image started to become clearer on both the monitor and the telescope itself.

"Question", Todd announced while not taking his eyes off the monitor, "I see a lot of snow which makes sense, but, if this really is the North Pole, I can't see anything to do with Santa or Christmas!"

"Oh, Todd, you're not going to see anything like that, for the same reason you don't see pictures of anything like that anywhere in books or on the internet, it's very well hidden", Noah said, rolling his eyes in his mind.

"Quite right, both of you, I do however have an idea which might help. It's a bit complicated but then all good science and magic is, just needs a bit more work on the telescope, I reckon, somewhere like Christmas land or whatever it may call itself will be hidden using a parallel dimension, which, ok, that's fine, now let me think, "Merlin wiped his brow, made his eyebrows twitch a little from concentrating on the problem quite hard then started to use his fingers to count, "hmm, carry two, add the five, allow for temporal displacement, assuming there's a wormhole (I believe the current terminology names it) somewhere in the vicinity, hopefully this side of the sun, erm, oh blast!"

"What's wrong, Merlin?" asked James.

"Ran out of fingers, toes don't work quite as well, don't suppose I could borrow yours temporarily could I?"

"Yes, of course" James agreed holding up his hands.

"Good lad, just the one hand should do, yes, perfect, right, back to the terminal".

Merlin returned to the terminal where he started to press a large number of buttons, some marked with unfamiliar markings, there weren't just numbers and letters of course, otherwise it would be nothing more than a computer keyboard. Everyone's eyes were now glued to the newly clearing image that was starting to appear. Now, it wasn't just snow, the partial green of trees could be seen, coloured lights. On both sides of a mountain. On one side was a large snow covered cabin with smoke coming out of a chimney, behind which stood what looked like a warehouse. The opposite side of the mountain was a large, very colourful building full of large windows, with children that could be seen running around outside the front, playing in the snow.

"I reckon that is the Rainbow quarter" Noah declared. Todd and James agreed

"Do you know this place, boys?" Merlin asked.. "Ah yes, of course you said about it when you met those other children in the games room, well that answers that!"

"Merlin, look! It's you!" James announced. Merlin could indeed be seen walking around the front of the Rainbow quarter giving the children a wide berth to avoid being hit by a stray snowball.

"So it is, how extraordinary, though not, thinking about it.So, I'm still there, glad I checked! I'm surprised I didn't mention it in my letter though I suppose at the time of writing I didn't know how long I'd be there? First thing first, I need to gather things and people so that everything is ready for when we leave. Talking of which, parents, I need to borrow your children if I may, discuss among yourselves I will answer any and all questions, next thing, Dave, I need to return to Oxford, if I can persuade you to pop me over there, I would have liked to do the journey by bus but time is against us so that will have to wait".

"I can happily pop you to Oxford, Merlin." Dave replied, "If you don't need to bring too much stuff back with you or indeed extra people, we can pop over there from here, as in from Dan's cave where we left the car".

"Most kind, if everyone is okay with that?"

The three boys were very enthusiastic about it, the adults seemed okay with the idea, Kelly had so many questions she didn't know where to begin. "Which reminds me, " Merlin thought, "where did those two naughty little owls get to? Anyone seen them?" Everyone shrugged or shook their head "Oh well, no matter I'm sure they'll show up somewhere, I was convinced they'd have stuck with you boys, I was wrong, clearly, ok, so, if I remember rightly, Oxford isn't too far from here, however, let's make our way back to Henrietta, there are bathrooms along the corridor we shall use in case anyone has a call of nature before we leave, nobody let me forget, I ought to send ahead a message to Bertha to let her know we'll be visiting and a few instructions.

"Merlin?" said Todd.

"Yes, lad?"

"Message Bertha!" Todd chuckled.

"Yes, good idea, I'll do that now before I forget, thank you"

"Welcome", Todd replied.

"Do bear with me everyone, if any one wants to look at the telescope, you're most welcome, I'll just press the reset button, you'll find controls on the right hand side to move around and zoom in and out etcetera". The adults started to form an orderly queue in front of the telescope while Merlin found his phone in his pocket and wrote a message to his daughter,

---

Hello, darling girl, it's Dad, just a quick message to say, I'm looking to pop over to you in a few hours probably, bringing the Swindon contingent with me as Dave has kindly agreed to give me a lift, can you see if my big ornate red candle is still there with you? Also, if any spirits are lurking, I need a quick word with Mr Dickens and if anyone is able to track down J.M.Barrie I would be most grateful, he's the chap that created Peter Pan etc, Hope all is well, say hello to everyone for me, much love, Dad.

"Right, all done, everyone follow me, back out the door, down the stairs and along the corridor we came in to from the hall", by this point Merlin realised he was over-talking and by now everyone had the right idea. Everyone followed him on the route he had just told them in more detail than was needed. He continued what felt like a guided tour, "okay as you can see we are approaching the large hall of doors again but even though instinct may tell you to turn right when we reach the outside of the games room, instead we are going to to take a narrow corridor in between the games room door and another". This they did, the narrow corridor had many bends in it with enough right turns to make you think you were likely going around in a large circle, but no.

"Is that the big hall of doors again in front of us?"James asked.

"Well spotted!" replied Merlin. "However, you will notice we are somewhat further up the hall now". As everyone stepped into the hall they realised they were now standing in front of the entrance door, Merlin made the door open to reveal a moonlit wood, "Here we go. Ah, there you are!" Mollie and Poem suddenly appeared in front of everyone as they flew out of the door. "We wondered where you'd got to! How come you are both covered in all those bright colours? Where on earth have you been?" Merlin asked.

"It's obvious, they've been to the Rainbow quarter!" Todd exclaimed.

"So you did follow the boys! Thought you might" said Merlin, amused. "Stick with us, now, don't go too far, I have an idea for you later". The two owls flapped their wings with excitement. Everyone followed Merlin outside and eventually back to Henrietta that was thankfully still parked exactly where they had left it. No reason for it to have moved of course, but you can never tell. Dave unlocked Henrietta to let people climb aboard.

"I'll be right with you everyone, just need to speak with Dan", said Merlin.

Completely unphased, Todd came up with the brilliant idea of climbing toward the back and reaching into the picnic basket from earlier and started to hand out chocolate ice creams for everyone, there was obviously huge variety available so some chose something different.Merlin stepped in to Dan's cave to be greeted first by Barry the badger. "Hello again, Merlin, are you all still here?"

"Only just," was Merlin's reply, "about to pop over to Oxford to see my daughter, and, others".

"Oh well that should be lovely, erm, I don't believe Dan is asleep, he's not snoring, he may just be resting, he does that"

"Yes, quite, well he's not young anymore I suppose, let's see." Merlin cautiously leaned further into the cave and called out in a dull whisper, "Dandelion?"

"Hmmm? What's that? Just checking the inside of my eyelids, is it time for a late supper?" Dan was confused in his sudden woken state.

"It's okay, it's just me, we're about to pop off to go find Bertha in Oxford.

"Oh okay, give her my love please"

"Certainly, oh, if you see those two pesky owls, tell them from me, I'll be back before they realise, so they're not to disappear. I'm far too busy to be tracking naughty owls as well as everything else. Also, fancy a another trip?

"Yes, of course, where to this time?"

"Well, when I get back to you, not sure how long I'll be away this time, hopefully only a matter of a few days, then I might need a lift to the North pole, there's someone there you need to meet, a few people actually".

"Okay, see you when you get back, I'll be here".

"Okay, quick ear rub?"

Dan didn't need asking twice, he leaned forward and Merlin performed the aforementioned rub of his left ear, the best thing in the world for a dragon. Merlin waved goodbye to everyone and went outside to join everyone in Henrietta, whereupon he was immediately given an ice-cream sandwich version of one of Todd's rainbow cookies.

"I've just thought of that!" Todd announced, "Tell me what you think".

"Oh I absolutely will, however my phone is vibrating, I forgot I'd set it to that, such a clever idea, okay, things in order, it's a message from Bertha, I can read and eat at the same time of course, Todd, this is magnificent, thank you".

"Welcome!" said Todd who was modestly in complete agreement.

Bertha's message read…

Hello Dad, Will and I are at the Eagle and Child pub with Katy and Sam, best to head for that if you can. I'll get Katy to keep an ear out for Mr Dickens and make enquiries about Mr Barrie. So looking forward to hearing about what you're up to, any more info on the glittery self addressed letter mystery? Love to the Swindon contingent, see you all later, B x

---

"Lovely, Bertha sends her love and says we're to make our way to the Eagle and child pub, please Dave".

"Okey dokey!" Dave replied, "I'll just put that into the satnav. Everyone got their seatbelts on I assume? If not, now's the time!" Dave turned the car around, and headed for Oxford. About an hour later, Dave said to Merlin, "Merlin, we're about ten minutes away, do you need to let Bertha know when we're arriving?"

"Good idea, Dave, thanks I'll give her a heads up"

Chapter Eleven

"Hello darling girl, just to let you know we'll be there in about ten minutes apparently, love Dad.

"Brilliant, Dad and everyone are nearly here, William, best to warn the others".

"On it", William replied and made his way over to Katy and Sam who were just coming out of the rabbit room, which you will remember was originally used by 'The Inklings' author group by Tolkien, Lewis et al.

"Hi guys, Bertie has heard from Merlin, he and the family from Swindon are arriving any minute".

"Well", Sam responded, "everything is ready, best get the headsets and everything ready too"

"Well ahead of you".

"I'll be over at the bar to make sure at least someone is there so customers don't think this place has been abandoned" Katy chipped in.

"Shall I join you to help?" Bertha asked.

"Please. The boys can be doing their thing and make sure everything is ready. Remember, if you need help communicating at any point I'm just over at the bar".

"It'll be ok, all headphones are charged and I've got a bank of chargers ready to go in the rabbit room itself in case", said Will.

Everything was ready, and if it wasn't, it was too late anyway as Merlin entered the pub followed by everyone else. Sam stepped forward to shake Merlin's hand, "Merlin! So good to see you again, feels like ages since you were last here".

"Even more so for me, much has happened since!"

"Hello everyone", Sam addressed the group that was now assembled just inside the entrance, "my name is Sam, if you'd like to follow me, we have a private space ready for you all just through here, I just hope there are enough seats, I can of course get more"

"There are only eight of us, "Merlin interrupted, including three young boys, I trust that isn't a problem?"

"No problem at all, and yes there are eight of you, but there is a queue of spirits going out the back door who are keen to speak with you, but they won't necessarily need seats, but it might be a nice touch".

"How interesting, tell me, where is Bertha?"

"She's behind the bar helping Katy, they both insisted on helping with that while Will and I prepped the room and helped you all out"

"Perfect"

"I'll swap out with them in a sec and send them over. I'm sure they'll want to see and meet everyone".

"Lovely, I hope you haven't been going to too much trouble"

"No no".

Sam made sure everyone was settled on the rabbit room, took drinks orders and made his way to the bar, grabbing Will on the way, upon reaching the bar, he said "ok ladies if you want to go and see everyone, they've arrived and are installed in the rabbit room, Will and I will take over the bar".

Both Katy and Bertha removed their aprons, handed them to their partners, thanking them and kissing each of them on the cheek. They made their way to the rabbit room to find Merlin who was the first to notice them, he stood and hugged them both. "Hello ladies, lovely to see you, Bertha, how are you, darling girl? Young Kathryn, sorry, I mean Katy, let me introduce you to everyone. This is Dave, his ancestor was a knight in old Swindon many centuries ago, he was the one that young Will contacted which led to the start of all our adventures. He is also an author and is helping me to document information about my adventures through time etcetera, he is also writing his own book and indeed another about King Arthur and the knights of the round table, with a little help from yours truly, I was actually there ya know!" Merlin said proudly. "Next up is Dave's wife, Gwen, who Bertha will agree bears a striking resemblance to my dear wife, Bertha's mother.

Then we have Noah and Todd, their two young sons. Boys, this is Katy, your 30 plus a few times great-grandmother, approximately, I don't expect that to sink in just now, it's quite complicated, she is in fact my grandmother" he said smiling, still quite mind blown by the fact himself. Noah stepped forward to say "can we hug you?"

"Of course you can, awww, sweet, both of you, I'm a big hugger, you obviously are too. And who is this?" Katy asked moving toward James.

"This equally brilliant young man, "Merlin began, "is James, he is Noah and Todd's cousin, I think that's right?" Merlin asked looking to the adults for confirmation. Everyone nodded.

"Hello Katy, I'm James' Mum, Kelly, we're not related to you guys, I'm Dave's cousin, and this is my husband, Ian, James' Dad. We have some interesting ancestors too, but we've never actually met any. I don't mean to be rude, but if you're meant to be Merlin's grandmother, how old are you? How old is your child or are your children?"

"It's okay, it's not rude, " Katy assured. "So I'm currently 24 years old. Sam, the guy who helped you when you arrived is my partner, He is the same age as me although I like to remind him a lot that I'm 4 months older! We don't have any children yet. We have been reliably informed that we will have a daughter in 2036 so only 13 years to wait", Katy laughed with a few visible tears in her eyes.

"Oh my, " Bertha suddenly exclaimed, laughing. "I've suddenly realised, that makes Sam my great-grandfather". Katy and Bertha hugged each other and laughed uncontrollably, collapsing onto two chairs together.

"So, Merlin, "Kelly started to address the old man, "you haven't been born yet? Isn't it somewhat risky meeting and interacting with the previous generations of your own family's timeline?"

"Brilliant observation, you're quite right, to make it worse it wasn't long ago I was sat in this very building, enjoying lunch with my great and indeed great-great grandmothers who were visiting young Kathryn over at the university. In fairness, meeting Katy was my greatest risk, because my Mother doesn't exist yet, but the further back you go, the risk of you not existing becomes less, whereas normally going forward in time is usually much lower risk. But this particular situation is quite unique. The odds of any of us meeting in the way we did is quite extraordinary.

"Sorry to interrupt, "Katy remarked, "Merlin, just to let you know that Bertie mentioned you wanted us to try and find Charlie and Mr Barrie?"

"Quite right, yes, can't think of any others at this time" Merlin replied.

"Okay, let me just go get Will, only both the men you requested have been found and are here waiting to talk with you".

"Brilliant, thank you, Katy, how exciting, Kelly, my dear I can read your face like a book, I suspect you have further questions, what a bit of luck I like questions a lot, except when my Great-great grandmother Julia interrogated me and figured out my true identity at impressive speed, so how can I help?".

"Ok, "Kelly began, "I heard names mentioned, Charlie? Mr Barrie? Bertie?"

"Yes indeed, I won't lie to you, Charlie is one Mr Charles Dickens, he of 'A Christmas carol among many others and Mr Barrie is Mr James Matthew Barrie, the creator of 'Peter Pan, Wendy Neverland, the lost boys, Tinkerbell etcetera' Oh and Bertie is a pet name given to my daughter Bertha who was just here with Katy, seems the youth of today aren't satisfied with their given names, they have to shorten it or make it truly unique".

"Ok, and how are you going to talk to Charlie and the other one?"

"James Barrie, well, young Will, who is Bertha's young gentleman friend, has very cleverly created special technology that you can wear on your head which enables you to both see and hear spirits from beyond the grave and communicate with them. Young Kathryn interestingly can hear spirits without help but she can't see them, so invention being the mother of necessity as it is said, one thing led to another and Will's genius, oh dear",

"What's wrong"?

"I just remembered my headset and everything, I have a bad feeling I left them in Marlborough".

"Don't worry, Merlin, " came Will's voice as he entered the room, "you'll be pleased to know that I'm well ahead of you, having gathered everyone's equipment from our first meet-up and rescuing yours from home, I have it all here, charging as we speak, and I may have taken the liberty of making some more, so we should be good to go. Let me grab yours for you and let me know if more are needed. Katy is just letting Charlie and James know you're here".

"Thanks, Will, brilliant as always".

"No problem, I'll be back soon with everyone's drinks".

"Okay everyone, may I have your attention"? Merlin began, "I am about to have an important meeting with two gentlemen, but this meeting is very different. It will require me to wear all this technological gear on my head because the men I am meeting are spirits from beyond the grave, I tend to avoid the term 'ghosts' out of respect for them. You are welcome to stay, on the understanding that if I need you to move or vacate your seat, please help me by doing so. Many thanks in advance. I shall sit over in the far corner leaving the rest of the room available and please, not too much noise, as good as this equipment is, it is sometimes difficult to hear spirits when they talk, though I admit that can likely be blamed on my advancing years. Wish me luck".

Merlin took up a seat at a small table in the back corner of the room, everyone else took a space at the larger table in the middle of the room. Dave convinced the three boys to help him over at the bar to grab drinks and take them to the room for everyone, saving Will a job.

"Thanks Dave, thanks boys, you didn't need to though, I was quite happy to bring it all in to you".

"No problem ", said Dave, "happy to assist".

Katy walked in just behind them approaching Merlin.

"Hi Merlin, are you ready I'll send them in to you" Katy asked.

"Yes, certainly".

Moments later, Merlin saw the two men enter the room.

"Good evening, gentlemen, do join me" said Merlin gesturing at two chairs placed opposite him on the other side of the table, "Charles, good to see you again, I would shake your hand but alas, nothing has been invented yet to allow me to do that, I wouldn't be at all surprised if young Will thinks of something one day, Mr Barrie I assume?" Merlin turned his attention to James Barrie being the man who entered the room with Charles.

"Yes indeed" he replied.

"Pleasure to meet you, Sir".

"Likewise" came the reply.

The three men sat.

"Right, I shall start as I was the one who asked for you both to be found. Mr Dickens, obviously we have met before, which I suppose in one way that makes this a little less odd. So, long story short, I was visiting an old friend in Southern France recently, upon my return, I received a very unexpected letter, unexpected because the letter was from myself, it didn't say where from though we now have reason to believe it came from the North Pole, cleverly deduced by young Todd over there the shorter of the three, he is a descendant of mine as is his older brother the larger of the three", Merlin pointed to where the three boys were sat drinking pint glasses of apple juice, looking as though they were slowly getting drunk."I have since proven the theory, so I need to visit the North Pole as soon as I can for several reasons, least of all to properly catch up with my own timeline, please tell me if nothing I say makes sense, I'm used to getting ahead of myself and others and just blurting out information as if everyone is already up to speed etcetera. Another thing mentioned was finding authors who have created stories with children in them, my other self, the one who sent the letter, seemed very keen to find you, Mr Barrie, something to do with your Lost Boys, however I'm afraid gentlemen, until I make my visit, I have no other information.Charles, I assume my request has something to do with the Cratchit children? Who else is known for authoring books about children?"

"Oh there's quite a few actually", Charles started to say, " Lewis Carroll of course",

"Ah yes of course, I've met him; surprised he wasn't a first thought when I wrote to myself in the letter. Anyone else"?

"Roald Dahl, very popular 20th century children's writer"

"Ok, so if you can draw up a list of people you can think of, can I assign one of you to follow me to the North Pole so that person can inform the others? I've yet to come up with a better plan of keeping contact with everyone"

"Sorry to interrupt",came Will's voice, "I didn't mean to overhear your conversation, but that does tend to happen in this pub, I just wanted to say I reckon I've got an idea for that, we can discuss when you're available, Merlin".

"Perfect, brilliant lad, looking forward to hearing it! Don't suppose anyone has seen or has the ability to get hold of Charles Dodgson? Also known as Lewis Carroll?"

"I'll ask Katy, give me a mo, all going well I assume?"

"Yes, the headset etcetera are working well, thank you for your continuing efforts, lad".

Will nodded politely and left the room, heading for the bar. He spotted Bertha and walked up to her, "Bertie, where's Katy?"

"I think she went with Sam in to the kitchen, what's up?"

"Nothing up, I have another find and summon request from Merlin".

"Ooh, ok, I'll shout through to her". Bertha turned away from the bar, opened a small hatch in the wall and spoke loudly through the opening, "Katy, sorry to interrupt anything, Will needs you".

"Oh, okay, send him through, we're just preparing food for table 21".

"Don't worry I heard you" came Will's voice, "hello both, Katy, Merlin says are we able to track down Lewis Carroll, he of Alice in Wonderland etcetera?"

"I'll put the word out", said Katy, "just need to sort this order, we had a spot of bother with the grill".

"Tell you what, I'll help Sam with that if you want to escape for a bit"

"Brill, " Katy left Sam and Will to conquer the grill and stepped back out to the bar area. She found Bertha again, "Don't suppose you know where John and or Jack are, do you?"

"I think I remember someone saying they *were* in the rabbit room, but that was ages ago" Bertha replied.

"No worries, I'll start in there, scream if you need me or get one of those two in the ktchen to come find me, shouldn't be long". Katy made her way into the rabbit room grabbed a spare headset and approached Merlin and his two guests, "evening, gentlemen, I understand you need to find Mr Carroll?"

"Thank you, lovely Katy, yes please, if at all possible?" Merlin answered.

"Have any of you seen John or Jack? Mr Tolkein or Mr Lewis"

"Hello Kathryn" came John Tolkein's voice from behind the table "Jack and I have loitered in here most of the evening, being nosey, how may we be of assistance?"

"Oh, hello John, "Katy said, turning round for the rare opportunity to actually see who she was talking to. Noah, Todd and James found it quite funny to see Katy wearing a virtual reality headset seemingly talking to herself, it occurred to all three of them that they would need to find out what she was doing and what it was all about.Katy continued, "If you've been loitering, you may be aware that for a reason I've yet to discover, Merlin needs to summon Lewis Carroll, he of Alice, Wonderland".

"Yes, yes we know who you mean, don't we Jack?" Jack, the preferred name of one C.S.Lewis nodded but seemed distracted. "Shouldn't be an issue, I'll press Miss Austen to put the word out immediately" John continued. "Are you alright, Jack?"

"What? Oh yes, just something caught my eye outside the window was all, gone now, still, nevermind. How are we getting on?" Jack answered.

"Young Kathryn was just asking after Lewis Carroll, "

"Oh, Carroll, yes, of course, what about him?"

"Merlin's asking after him",

"Oh, wonder what that's about, best to ask Jane if she can find him",

"Yes indeed, already ahead of you on that one, was just about to pop over to the college to enquire".

"Very good, I shall remain here in case anything is needed".

"Jack, quick word if I may?" came the voice of Charles Dickens,

"Certainly, best of British, John, catch up with you later",

"Righto, I'll be back fairly soon all being well, Kathryn, make sure Jack doesn't start on the mead, he suffered greatly in the days when he could physically drink, but that was some time ago, dread to think what would happen now".

Katy smiled, Jack coughed, Merlin sniggered. Jack joined the small table with the others. Charles continued,

"Now, Jack, am I right in thinking that your Narnia chronicles involved children? I'm ashamed to say I've never read them".

"Ah yes, of course, " Merlin began to interject with his own narrative, "I'm familiar with your work, Sir, now don't tell me, Peter, Susan Edmund and Lucy…..Pevensie? I believe anyway.

"Yes, exactly, I'm so excited that you know my work Mr, erm…"

"Just Merlin is fine it has only ever been that" he smiled.

"\yes, of course, Merlin, brilliant, consider your hand shaken".

"Likewise".

Merlin went on to explain what had happened so far to bring Jack up to date and tell of the need to go to the North Pole.

It suddenly occurred to Katy who was back at the bar with the others and indeed Merlin who was still wearing his headset equipment, that it had become quite noisy in the pub for a usually quiet evening. Merlin excused himself, promising to return soon and made his way to the bar.

"Aha, Katy, am I right in thinking the number of patrons in this venue has increased somewhat? Only I can barely hear the people next to me".

"Yes, Merlin it has, it is rather noisy. I'm glad I'm not the only one who noticed, the amount of living customers is currently less than twenty which includes you all in the rabbit room, yes, Sir, how may I help?" Katy enquired off to one side, she put on her headset too to be able to see, in front of her was a smart young gentleman dressed in clothes of the Victorian era.

"Am I correct in assuming I am addressing a Miss Kathryn?"

"Yes, I'm Katy". Merlin, who could obviously see the young man, suddenly declared, "Lewis!, Is that you old friend?"

"Merlin! So good to see you, I got word you were here looking for me?"

"Yes quite right, erm, Lewis this is Katy, my daughter Bertha's friend, Katy this is Charles Dodgson, better known as Lewis Carroll, Lewis, follow me I have some people I'd like you to meet, Katy, thank you for your help, hope you're not too run off your feet with all these people, could I trouble you for a sherry, just to keep out the cold you understand, old bones aren't overly good at insulating".

"Yes of course, I'll get one sent in to you, can't wait to hear all about this evening's goings-on".

Lewis followed Merlin to the rabbit room whereupon, introductions were made by Merlin for the three authors. Lewis Carroll was also brought up to speed

"So I hope this doesn't come across as rude at all, "Lewis Carroll began, "I have a question which I'm reasonably confident I already know the answer to, but something confuses me. Mr Dickens and Mr Barrie, I assume you are both spirits like myself, we tend to recognise our fellow deceased brethren easily. But Merlin, you're different, It's almost as though you're alive and breathing".

"I AM alive and breathing," Merlin said louder than he intended, which made a lot of people jump. "I am not deceased as yet, nor do I intend to be anytime soon, I'm simply old".

"You must be impossibly old, you were old when we knew each other in life"

"I turned 794 this past June!"

"You still don't look a day over 80"

"Most kind, my great great grandmother said exactly the same thing in this very public house just recently, must be true, independent sources and all that, and if you remember me well, you'll also remember my dislike of the word impossible, it's unlikely I grant you but I am quite literally living proof of it's possibility".

"Astonishing".

"You now know as much as we do, dear chap, I received a letter from myself requesting Mr Dickens, Mr Barrie in particular, but the running theme seems to be children, which is why I have also wrangled Mr C.S.Lewis here, and then of course I thought of your good self or rather Mr Dickens did, so we put the word out to track you down, thinking of course of your stories of young Alice, not so young by now though I would imagine".

"Ah dear Alice, no indeed, she passed some, ooh, nearly 90 years ago at the grand age of (*not as impressive as your good self of course*) 82. Do you still have the mirror?"

"Oh yes, that has become more useful than any of us could have imagined, always in use! Whatever became of Doodle?"

"The dodo? Well as you're aware he became a part of my books, but can now be found in the Natural History museum in London, the only example they have of one it seems".

"Good heavens, I remember seeing a good number of them running all over the beaches of Mauritius. Such a shame they became extinct, charming bird if a little loud at times".

"Of course you of all people have the power to bring them back again"

"I'm afraid not old friend, not my place to interfere with God and nature, or indeed anyone else's place to do so, We've just got to assume there's a good reason for it all or some bigger plan we're yet to understand. If we start bringing creatures out of extinction from the past, we would be playing God, taking matters into our own hands which could cause all manner of chaos. Which reminds me, gentlemen I need to bring in my daughter's young man to meet you all, he is the brilliant mind which created this thing I'm wearing on my head which allows me to see and hear you and any other spirits, I'm confident you'll all get along very well. Talk amongst yourselves, shan't be long". Merlin made his way to the bar again, he found Bertha and Katy.

"Hello ladies, I need to find Will, Bertha you may want to join us too, some interesting people to meet over in our room".

"Say no more, Dad, we'll be over shortly", said Bertha.

"Perfect, many thanks".

"Oh, Merlin, do you still want that sherry?" Katy asked, "I can get you one now if you like".

"Oh, yes, lovely, thank you".

Katy sorted a sherry out for Merlin, meanwhile, Bertha was talking to Will and Sam explaining the situation.

"Don't worry, " Sam started to say, "Katy and I have got this, the living are starting to leave anyway so in many ways this place is becoming a lot easier to manage, apart from answering questions and I've got Katy for that, we're all good, see you soon". Sam started to subtly encourage Bertha and Will on their way, away from the bar and towards the rabbit room. "Katy, " he smiled, "you and I have the bar and kitchen, but there is literally nothing to do, so take the weight off, have a drink and sit at the bar while I do a bit of till admin", he escorted Katy over to the barstools and lifted her ontoz one of them sitting her in front of where he knew he'd be going behind the bar. Bertha and Will made their way into the Rabbit room, both grabbed a headset with the headphones and Will pulled out a vacant seat for Bertha before fetching his own. They were now sat with various family but at a table with Merlin and four deceased authors.

"Welcome, "Merlin began, "gentlemen, allow me to introduce my daughter Bertha and her young man, Will, as you will remember me saying just a few moments ago, Will is the brilliant mind that invented a way of us living folk seeing those of you who have, 'moved on', is that the right way to say it? I always feel I'm about to insult folk".

"Salutations to you both, allow me to introduce myself, I am Charles Dickens, Bertha is it? I see a resemblance between you and your Father, I assume you get your beautiful eyes from your Mother? No offence meant or indeed taken, Merlin", Dickens twinkled.

"Certainly none taken, Sir, she has indeed inherited her looks from her Mother who was equally beautiful when I met her, she would have been around Bertha's age".

"Captivating", Lewis Carroll chipped in, introducing himself.

"I suppose I'm next, " said Jack, clearing his throat more out of habit than actual need. "I'm Jack, we've met before, charmed".

"Hello everyone" were the only words that formed logically to Bertha's mind to say.

"And this brilliant young man is the aforementioned Will. Now, without wishing to put you on the spot, you mentioned earlier, you may have dreamt up a solution to my problem of communicating quicker with spirits at a distance?"

"Er,yup, without making this sound like it does I've been spending a lot of time with Jane, Austen, purely because I wanted to understand more about how spirits communicate with each other and I had other ideas of things I wanted to solve and invent, including spirit's ability to consume food and drink, though I'm told they don't experience what we would consider to be hunger or thirst just 'cravings', from memories of when they were alive…"

"Very true", Jack agreed, "So for example, right now I have no thirst but I'd give almost anything for a pint of mead, but sadly, the memory is all I have".

There was an awkward silence broken eventually by Merlin, "carry on lad, what are your thoughts?"

"Well, it occurs to me that the usual way of forced communication, by which I mean, making yourself heard over a great distance to a specific recipient without the need to be in the same room or just space is to approach the problem from a slightly different angle. Sorry I'm mumbling".

"You sound like Dad", Bertha said, squeezing Will's hand affectionately.

"I don't mumble, do I?" Merlin retorted.

Bertha simply looked at her Father and smiled warmly.

Chapter Twelve

"Aaaanyway..." Will continued, "So, then I got to thinking about gps trackers, for those unfamiliar, this technology allows someone to have a small bit of tech either attached to them or inside a vehicle or someone's pocket, worn as a piece of jewellery even, and other people can then see precisely where they are from anywhere on the planet, so I figured, surely, this technology can also incorporate some sort of communication device, for example gps is used on mobile phones a lot these days so that sorts out the communication issue all in one place, however, spirits can't really use physical devices, yet, however, I remember my Dad talking about a simple intercom system he rigged up at his home when he was a teenager, which allowed two-way communication, so one end had the ability to listen to whatever the microphone the other end was picking up, both ends had the ability to summon the other by pressing a button which would make a noise for the other end of the system, alerting them. What I'm saying is, it seems there is a large screen TV stored away for when this pub hosts a sports night or some sort of TV based event. We could put the TV in here, we can bring up a map on it which will show Merlin's exact location via tracker device which I will make sure is with him, He will also be able to send messages to us that will also show up on the TV, all using most likely and logically from my point of view, mobile phones. For those unfamiliar with the erm mobile phones, or indeed telephones, apologies, I'm yet to learn what people are familiar with so bear with me, a phone is an invention whereby two parties or indeed years later after being invented multiple parties as long as each party had a phone, everyone concerned could talk to each other over long distances,each phone had an earpiece with which to hear the other user or users and a mouthpiece to reply. Then many decades later, technology allowed the same idea but the phones could not only fit in a pocket but could be carried around and didn't require wiring to link the parties together, hence the now very familiar term 'wireless' and these devices became known as 'mobile' phones, in my mind Merlin would have one with him, I would connect one to a screen or monitor here which will show us where he is and any messages he sends through, that's the theory. The other lovely thing about it is, it doesn't require anyone to have to physically interact with anything, with the possible exception of replying to messages which, if I also arm Merlin with a headset which I will do of course in which case you can simply go to him and talk to him in person (*so to speak*) as you'll be able to see on a large map exactly where he is. And given we'll have the large screen here, there can be any number of you in here watching his progress without disturbing the ongoing everyday operation of the pub and if any help is needed, you'll have myself, Bertie, Katy or Sam around, usually at the bar to assist you". Will sat back, visibly relaxed, "Any questions?"

There was an audible murmuring among everyone present. Suddenly, Betha felt someone tapping her on the shoulder. It was Noah, she turned to hug him, "hello you, how have you been getting on? How's school?"

"Hi, I'm okay, school is, meh, "Noah shrugged his shoulders with the word meh to denote school was neither good or bad just somewhere in the middle, tolerable. He beckoned Berha forward so he could whisper in her ear, " I've got a question for Will".

"Oh, okay, William, a quick question from Noah".

Will swung round. "Hey dude, you're taller again I reckon, what's the question?"

"Well, " Noah began, "yeah, taller again, Mum says I'm costing her a lot with shoes and stuff like school uniform, I can't help it, she's the one feeding me", once those within earshot of Noah's voice had stopped chuckling, his Mum was within earshot but wasn't chuckling, she simply smiled and nodded in agreement. Noah continued, "I heard you talking about giving Merlin a small tracker for travelling to the North pole, just wanted to say that I'd love to help with things if I'm allowed, also, would I be allowed to try one of the headsets you've all been wearing? I didn't mean to hear conversations but I think someone, maybe Merlin said that it helps you see ghosts? As long as it's not scary, I'd love to try it", Noah was starting to talk quicker to get all his thoughts out.

"Hang on, slow down, " Will chuckled as he turned towards Gwen and Dave. "Guys, is Noah okay to try some of this headgear?"

"Only if we can too" Gwen and Dave said simultaneously.

"Yes of course, "Will said with a smile, "I'll sort Noah out first, right dude, just like a VR headset, in fact that's exactly what it is but it's using more augmented reality than anything so you'll still be able to see us all, nothing scary in there, you'll just see more people than you can normally, and these headphones will help you hear all the new people but you'll still be able to hear us too, okay?"

"Ok, "Noah replied apprehensively. He looked around himself and saw three extra men sat with Merlin, there were a few people outside a window too but that didn't register as anything odd in his mind, he looked at Will. "Okay, all looks good, so, where are these ghosts at?"

Will leaned closer and said quietly, "I think they prefer to be called spirits, just a heads up".

"Oh ok, sorry, understood".

"Let me introduce you". Will turned towards the gentlemen at Merlin's small table, "Hello again all, I'd like to introduce my 'sort of' cousin, Noah.

"Good evening, young man" said a bearded man, "I am Charles Dickens, you may call me Charles".

"The author?" Noah asked.

"The same. We're all authors at this table"

"I'm J.M.Barrie, "the next man offered up.

"And I'm C.S.Lewis, please, call me Jack".

"Narnia!" Noah exclaimed loudly, pointing, followed by his signature giggle, "sorry",

"Not at all, delighted that such a young person has heard of me".

"I have a question," Noah stated.

"Please, fire away"

"Why 'Jack'?"

" I'm afraid that's a long story, are you sure you want to know?"

"Yes please".

"Very well, bring your seat round here next to me and I'll tell you"

Noah did as requested, and sat between Jack and Merlin but not before giving Merlin a quick hug, which was reciprocated, "Merlin, something smells funny, that's not me being rude, it's a slightly sweet smell" Noah said.

"Oh, perhaps it's my drink? Smell it".

Noah did so, "yes that's it, what is it?"

"It's called sherry, try a little"

"No thanks, hello Jack"

"Hello lad, okay then, " Jack went on to explain how when he was a young lad, younger than Noah, he had a dog called Jack, but sadly that dog died and he felt he always wanted to hold on to the name as his own in his dog's memory. Noah then went on to explain that he had a dog when he was young, but his was called Jackrum, named after a character in a book by an author named Terry Pratchett. However he never felt compelled to use the name Jackrum as his own, a bit too unusual perhaps. They both felt they had bonded over their love of their dogs so this was a great introduction for Noah to the spirit world and Will's invention. They continued to chat aimlessly, meanwhile Will fitted Gwen and Dave with headsets and headphones. Merlin insisted on doing the introductions this time. "Gentlemen, this lady is called Gwen, she is my great granddaughter by 30 or so generations, this is her husband Dave, and they are parents to Noah and young Todd over there, with Todd is another fine young man by the name of James and James' parents are Kelly and Ian. Kelly is Dave's cousin making James, Noah and Todd's 2nd cousin, I believe, I always get a bit confused by how that works with family relationships but I think I'm right, Gwen, for your point of reference bares a striking resemblance to my wife, even more so than Bertha, my wife is also by pure coincidence named Gwendolyn, Gwen you must tell me about your family history at some point, and how is Zoe, sorry Will, she's your mother, it would be best to ask you, I did see her recently as you'll remember, didn't see your Dad though, he was well the last time I saw him however".

"Mum and Dad are both doing great, Merlin", Will answered.

"Fantastic, right, okay, in no particular order other than potentially alphabetical, we have Mr J.M.Barrie, Mr Charles Dickens, Mr Charles Dodgson, better known as Lewis Carroll and with Noah is C.S.Lewis known to his friends and family as 'Jack'".

"I'll explain later Mum", Noah said.

"Right okay,"Gwen began, "lovely to meet you all, Mr Barrie, I feel I need to address you first, I have a great fondness for your work, my parents would often take me to see the statue of Peter Pan in Kensington gardens. I also own a copy of Peter Pan containing original illustrations by Arthur Rackham."

"Thank you for your kind words, madam I do love that statue in Kensington gardens, I have returned to it many times and Mr Rackham's extraordinary talent was a thrill to have commissioned alongside my work", was the author's response.

A story Jack was telling Noah about his original pronunciation of the name Aslan the lion from Narnia which he had to make sure was pronounced differently so as not to cause offence had caused Noah to laugh so hard he nearly spat apple juice everywhere.

"You alright, Noah?" Dave asked.

"Sorry, "Jack chipped in, "my fault, told him a funny story, funnier than I thought it might be if I'm honest, been a long time since I was his age".

"I'm okay, "said Noah catching his breath, but started laughing again, he was fooling nobody.

"Can I be rude and just catch everyone's attention please?" said Will to the room. "Firstly a question to anyone who heard me talking before about mobile phones and tracking Merlin on his trip to the North pole, does everyone agree it's a good idea?" At which point there was a very positive response from everyone, "lovely, great, thanks, and one last thing, any more drinks?"

Most people wanted refills which made things easier, less to remember, and the young boys were getting hungry, Bertha suggested crisps from the bar which also got a positive response. Bertha and Will both returned to the bar to sort the orders out, Katy and Sam were standing guard behind the bar in deep conversation about something but had their minds interrupted by Bertha audibly running through a list of drinks and snacks from memory. Seeing their confusion, Will offered up, "these are orders from the gang in the rabbit room",

Guessed that, " Katy said, "okay, this is what we're used to doing, so let's sort it. Bertie, if it's all in your head we can station each of us at different points of the bar, make it quicker".

"Good idea, Sam and Will, I need a beer and a lager shandy, Katy, three large apple juices and I'll recharge Dad's sherry", Bertha blurted out at speed, "oh and whoever, a cider and a large orange juice, then it's an assortment of crisps just bung a variety of packs in a basket I reckon". Within a matter of minutes all orders were delivered. After which Will told Sam of his idea to put the large TV in the rabbit room so a crowd could track Merlin easily and privately from confused eyes.

"Another moment of genius, mate, I can help with that, I'm sure Katy will be happy to be on hand to navigate the tech if needed, but you'll be around I'm sure, all going well in there I take it?" Sam asked.

"Yes, mate, all is well. I forget what an absolute legend Merlin is sometimes, he'll suddenly come out with something which reminds you he's not just a doddering old man from a forgotten moment in the distant past, brilliant, anything you need help with?"

"Nah, there's nobody left in here, the night is young however, that could all change".

"Alright, no worries, you know where I am if you need me, we should look at rigging up the TV in the next few days, think the old man is eager to get cracking"

"Cool, we can make that happen".

Will walked back to join the others. Merlin approached Katy, "Katy, do you remember the very ornate candle you had in a box of other candles in your dormitory over at the college?"

"Yes, of course",

"Do you still have it and is it accessible?"

"Yes it's still in the box, you made a point of asking me to keep it safe and to never light it, don't you remember?"

"I don't but I was absolutely right and thank you for remembering and keeping it safe, we may need it, I'll explain that a bit better another time"

"No problem, let me know when you need it".

"Thanks. Right, next victim, Dave!"

"I heard my name?" Dave responded.

"Yes, hope I'm not interrupting, just need to let you know the plan in my head, "

"Not at all, what are your thoughts?"

"Well I've mostly got things tied up here, the next stage is to go to the North Pole, I've yet to figure the best way of getting there, especially with the children and their Mums, can't expect them all to hang on to a flying dragon, no matter how fun it sounds in principle, and I can't expect said dragon to carry us all over two and a half thousand miles both ways with potential repeat trips, I do have a theory though, as always,now tomorrow, could I trouble you to whisk me over to my dragon again? We can do a lone trip if you wish, at any hour, I'm not fussy".

"Yes, certainly, shall we pop over early in the morning, we can get a little rest tonight, pop over and potentially get some breakfast either en route there or back".

"Perfect! Many thanks, next port of call is young Kelly, Hello you two," Merlin said moving in the general direction of Kelly and Ian, " how are you both getting on? Don't want you to feel excluded, fancy meeting the others?"

"Which others are they, Merlin?" Kelly asked.

"Well, I know you'll think I'm mad, perhaps more mad than you originally thought, but I have managed to assemble a few key people for my upcoming quest, four significant authors from the 19th and 20th centuries, namely, now keep an open mind, my dear, on that table there we have Charles Dickens, Lewis Carroll, J.M.Barrie and young Noah looks like he's talking to himself, but no, next to him is one C.S.Lewis. I could introduce you if you wish?"

"Oh Merlin, I know you perhaps consider that I came down with the last shower of rain but, this would be a bit of a leap, even for me, I know I've witnessed some amazing and for my little brain, some unexplainable things today but, talking to dead authors is a step too far, sorry I can't play along with that, I don't want to sound like the party killer".

"Understood, if you change your mind and curiosity overrides your basic desire to go with logic, you know I'm just across here with Noah and what must look like to the straight-thinking sensible eye, an old man having a senior moment, talking to himself".

"Sorry Merlin, I truly believe that you believe in what you're saying, thank you for being so lovely today, that whole thing with the picnic basket in the car was truly brilliant and as for the shopping mall and the observatory in that big building in the middle of nowhere, I must admit does make me want to give you the benefit of the doubt but my brain and heart are still adjusting".

"Not to worry, honestly, I'm not offended, it's entirely up to you, I'm not doing all this to try and make you look a fool, I promise", he smiled while trying his level best not to make his smile look mocking.

"He's really not, Kel, honestly, "Dave said trying to encourage Kelly to join in, "Gwen's been bending J.M.Barrie's ear out of shape, talking about his Peter Pan stories, big fan apparently, nothing to lose, you just need one of these headsets, go on, give it a go".

Kelly pulled a face which was a rich mixture of confusion and being unsure.

"Perhaps if I might try it? Would that be ok?" Ian asked.

"Good man, yes of course, "Merlin responded.

Will overheard and made a point of fetching Ian his own headset and headphones, "here you go, Ian, nice to meet you both, by the way, I'm Will, Bertha's other half, my overall connection with Swindon party is complicated, I'm usually based in Marlborough. I can confirm what Dave just said, and the four authors Merlin mentioned are not the only ones, we had a pub full of them last time Merlin was here".

"Fascinating!" said Ian who had taken the liberty of putting on his headset and could see everyone gathered at Merlin's table. "I have to say, I'm aware of the technology advances with holographic imagery, but this is very real, I recognise Charles Dickens immediately, I've seen old photos, "

Charles Dickens turned his head towards Ian to say, "hello, yes, I heard my name, you are correct it's me". Ian did what he could not to scream and perhaps leave the room, but that was quite a moment. Ian tried to convince Kelly that there was definitely something to look at and it's all very interactive, he was unsure if it was real even if Charles Dickens did turn round and answer his name, "technology is scarily clever , as is the power of artificial intelligence, you'd have to try it for yourself and make your own mind up" he said.

Kelly's curiosity got the better of her so she reluctantly allowed Will to fit her out with a headset and earphones, after the initial shock of seeing all the extra faces, her first port of call was Lewis Carroll, who she recognised very quickly. At this point, Sam entered.

"Hello folks, just to let you know that it doesn't matter how late it gets, I've become used to doing regular late 'lock-in's recently, no other living soul can come in now, we have the whole place to ourselves, I might lower the lighting in the main part of the building just to avoid too much attention from outside, nothing to worry about, Will, could I grab a headset too, because we tend to get latecomers, no idea what I did with mine".

"No worries, "Will responded, "I grabbed yours earlier to charge up, I'll just fetch it for you, we should start labelling them all, always fancied an excuse to get a labelling gun".

Gwen tapped Dave on the arm to get his attention, "I'm not suggesting we leave now, but it's been a long day and the boys shouldn't be out too late, with Merlin here I guarantee more things we need to get our rest in for".

"Agreed, " Dave responded, "I've agreed to drive Merlin back up to Dan's cave in the morning, and not forgetting Kelly Ian and James still need to get all the way back over to Surrey, though it does occur to me we have enough room, if they would prefer to stay at ours tonight".

"I'll ask them in a sec, Kelly seems to have got past her scepticism with Lewis Carroll, Todd and James seem to be okay sat over there plotting something no doubt, Noah seems fine, all is well"said Gwen who felt relaxed again without a hint of anxiety.Everything from that point seemed to slot into place, Kelly and Ian both agreed to stay over in Swindon at which point Todd and James were found asleep holding a side of Todd's Nintendo hand held games device each, the decision was made to start to wrap the evening up.

"Well, "Merlin began to address the gathered spirits and anyone who was listening, "this has been a true pleasure yet again, I have of course got plans to return as soon as the current plan has been seen through. I have yet to experience the joys of cross-country bus travel so before all this North Pole business, I had intended to grab a bus here from Swindon. Merely a moved feast, to paraphrase a phrase of old, by which I mean, it can happen at any time. I suggest we reconvene here in the future and I will do the best I can to keep you all up to date on my travels and adventures and hope you'll all be watching me on Will's marvellous tracking system. I want to thank my daughter Bertha, her Will, Katy and of course, Sam, for looking after us all so well this evening, looking forward to doing this all again".

A rousing round of "Hip hip, hooray" was started by Charles Dickens.

"Most kind". Merlin almost blushed. He turned to Bertha. "Bertha my darling, would you consider coming to the North pole too with me and the others?Namely the three young boys and their mothers, only if one of my theories is correct, you'll want to be there too. As would Katy, in fact, oh dear, yes, I hadn't thought this through fully, not even there yet and I don't want to drag people all that way for nothing, though the me that sent the letter was keen to mention the children, so I feel that's all above board, if you'd like to join me and the rest if I can convince them, then I'd need you to be up at Dan's cave for midday if you can?".

"I'll talk to William, Dad, I'm sure it will be fine, and I'd be another adult for the children, so that would make sense".

"Quick interruption, "came Will's voice, "couldn't help overhearing, can't speak for the other two but I'll make sure Bertie is there tomorrow if that's what she wants to do, I'll be here with Sam to help with whatever, again with making sense, if the tech needs a helping hand, it's best if I was here, plus which it will distract me while Bertie's away", Will held and squeezed Bertha's hand to let her know he was being genuine about it being okay if she went".

"I'll talk to Katy", said Bertha. Think I'd be better at convincing her. Bear with me".

Bertha returned barely a few minutes later, "All sorted. So, William, here's the plan. Katy is getting public transport over to Marlborough college in the morning, then if you could take me up to the cave and come back to pick Katy up, drop her off. Then if you're able to pop back here to help Sam set up the tracking stuff, us girls will have our phones of course, so we can all communicate easily hopefully".

"Sounds good to me, "Will answered, "I doubt phone reception will be overly great if available at all in the North pole, guess we'll find out, your Dad will have tracking on him, I'm still researching it all, I promise to have it all ready for tomorrow, we should probably head back, everyone needs their rest I reckon". This was agreed upon by everyone in earshot, Will and Bertha jumped on Will's bike and headed back to Marlborough, Sam and Katy were the last to leave so they could lock up. Sam made a point of putting the large screen tv in the rabbit room ready for the next day. They headed back to the college to sleep, far more comfortable than under the bar or anywhere else in the pub, plus it had the added advantage of a spare bed if Bertha was in Marlborough, everyone else climbed in to Henrietta and headed back to Swindon, the two youngest had been carefully poured in to their seats so remained asleep for the most part, as usual, Noah was last man standing, demanding a last apple juice before bed and trying to make sure he didn't miss anything by going to bed straight away, especially as a conversation had started in the car which grabbed his attention.

Merlin began by saying, "thank you all for being there this evening and humouring an old man's crazy whims, I have a proposition for Kelly in particular. This may be a bit of a long shot given your reticence for other aspects of my magic, hobbies, lifestyle, general 'goings-on', however, nothing ventured' as they say, tomorrow, I hope to travel to the North pole, I have as good as convinced Gwen to come with me, because I'm very much hoping to take the children with us, that's an important part. I, of course, would not dream of suggesting that young James come with us alone, but if you were to join us? Ian, Dave is staying behind in Swindon and he has their good friends Zoe and Chris just over in Marlborough, should anything be needed, they being young Will's parents, Oh, one last detail, my daughter Bertha and young Katy will be coming along too if that helps sway you towards the positive at all, what do you think? Tell you what, don't answer straight away, I'm merely planting the seed of thought, sleep on it, Dave has kindly agreed to drive me over to the dragon's cave again first light in the morning, then I've told Bertha and indeed now Katy to meet us there for midday, so I reckon, those coming will need to be ready for about 11am. Think on it, talk to Ian, talk to Gwen, Dave, the boys too obviously, though they have a wonderfully adventurous spirit, all of them so I doubt they'll require much convincing".

"And just how are you looking to get us all to the North pole?" Kelly asked, "and surely we'd need warm clothing, we all know we'd be fed with you around so that's not an issue" she was almost talking herself into the idea but shook herself out of it until she'd had the chance to analyse every aspect of the idea".

"Well, to answer your question about travelling tomorrow"Merlin answered, I believe I can put your mind at rest by telling you that I've scrapped the idea of using my dragon, I have a theory that I will be testing when I return to the cave in the morning, if I'm right, it will be an instantaneous affair with little effort and strain to anyone or any thing". Once back in Swindon, everyone was ordered to make themselves comfortable in the living room with a round of hot chocolate drinks, Merlin got the fireplace lit and once they had sunk their hot chocolates, the boys were put to bed, Noah included. Dave showed the boys that underneath the bottom bunk was a clever built-in feature which pulled out to reveal a third bed, an impulse buy from when the boys were much younger and would now serve its purpose to allow the three of them to share a room.

"Now no arguments, please figure out quickly and sensibly who is to sleep where, James, let me show you where the bathroom is in case you need it in the night", said Dave.

"I'll show you where stuff is, "Todd offered, he and James disappeared down the hallway where Todd opened a door to reveal the main upstairs bathroom revealing the all important toilet.Dave meanwhile made up Merlin's bed in the office room, and downstairs, Gwen demonstrated her own magic by changing one of the sofas in to a double bed. "Kelly, Ian, this is for you to sleep on if you're okay with it, Merlin, I can hear Dave sorting your bed out upstairs".

"Lovely, I think I shall turn in and pop up and help if needed", thanks again everyone, see you all at some point tomorrow no doubt, sleep well all".

"Night, Merlin", came from everyone.

"I'll just pop my head in on the boys when I go up, no doubt the owls will have already done so but I like to make sure", said Gwen.

"The owls?" asked Kelly.

"Yes, Mollie and Poem from before over at the cave, they fly over to say goodnight, it's very sweet".

"Perhaps I should look in on James, too, I'll pop up with you if that's okay?"

"Yes of course".

The two women made their way upstairs, popped their heads round the boys' bedroom door. James had taken the spare pullout bed next to the bottom bunk, all three of them were asleep already. The owls had already dimmed the light but were nowhere to be seen, presumably already on their way back to the dragon's cave.

"Goodnight ladies", came Merlin's voice from behind them, "sorry, didn't mean to startle you, Gwen, tell Dave not to be afraid to wake me in the unlikely situation that he's awake before I am. I'm quite excited, I do love an adventure".

"Night Merlin", said Gwen giving him a kiss on the cheek.

Gwen and Kelly said goodnight and parted ways at the top of the stairs, both Dave and Ian were asleep just like the boys.

Chapter Thirteen

In a matter of just a few hours, sunlight was starting to spill into Merlin's room/the office. Gwen for some reason had woken up a half an hour earlier and was already downstairs, Kelly had woken too and the two of them could be found nattering over a coffee in the kitchen.

"I haven't really slept, if I'm honest," said Kelly, "I'm perfectly rested and awake though, mind was racing a bit overnight, Ian was no help, he'd fallen asleep, so any hope of a chat ended before it started, Oh Gwen, I'm on a fence with it all, should we go?"

"Well I'm going, "Gwen answered, "wherever we end up, I trust Merlin completely, I can't give up the opportunity, I'd go out of my mind if I stayed here, I have to know what this is all about".

"Me too, but do I put myself and James through it? Then in turn Ian would be worried I expect and would have to put up with us going on about it once we're back"

"Well, all I know is, travels with Merlin is always interesting and surprising, I think the boys are all already sold on the idea, and given the few clues we've been given so far, I imagine Father Christmas will have something to do with it, North pole, glitter in Merlin's letter, the request for children, nothing more magical than the idea of Christmas with the big man himself, "

"Yes, true, but, "

"But?"

"Oh come off it, Gwen, you know what I'm going to say"

"Well, I for one, have always believed in him, but then I've experienced stuff with him first hand, I must admit I was a bit apprehensive when he first appeared upstairs out of the blue. Let's put it this way, I'll be there, so will Bertie and Katy, both of which are our ancestors and Merlin won't let anything happen to either of them because the implications on his own timeline are mind-boggling".

"You sound like him" Kelly Laughed.

"Well it's true, If Katy really is his grandmother, if anything happens to her he won't exist and none of the events of this past weekend will have happened, No Bertha, no me, neither of the boys would exist, Dave would have maybe married someone else, complicated isn't it, so I'm all for making the most of this unique situation before something goes wrong and it's all erased from existence, not that I think it will, but it wouldn't take much".

There's a possibility that Kelly detected a certain emotion coming from Gwen and so put her arms around her and hugged her tightly, "thank you, you've helped me decide, I wouldn't want things to be different either, I'll come with you if only for company, us girls need to stick together". Gwen hugged tightly back.

"Thank you, I have a good feeling about this".

With excellent timing and perhaps a small case of over-hearing, Merlin wandered in, "Aha, good morning, ladies, no Dave yet? Sun's up!"

"Morning Merlin, coffee? Apple juice? Something a bit stronger?" Gwen asked.

"I think coffee is order of the day today, I need to be alert for it!"

"Coming right up".

"Merlin, " Kelly began, "just to let you know I've decided to come along with you and the others to the North pole and James of course, if that's ok"

"Yes, of course it is, how lovely, everything is falling into place, marvellous".

"This should wake the men up", Gwen announced, "I'm going to cook up some bacon and sausages, this is 'my magic', "she laughed. Sure enough, the smell of cooking meat travelled through the house along with the smell of freshly brewed coffee, Ian and Dave blearily almost walked into each other trying to both occupy the kitchen doorway.

"Ah! Merlin! You're up, I wondered where you were, I went to your room to wake you, but you beat me to it", said Dave.

"Indeed I did, morning, gentlemen, I trust you both slept well?"

Both men agreed they had.

"Gwen, "Dave started, "another miraculous smell of fried breakfast, Merlin any objection to a quick breakfast before we head off?"

"Not at all, I was thinking the same, smells wonderful doesn't it? I think we all need it today, now, what can I do to help?"

"Tell you what, here is a container of cutlery, "Gwen remarked handing over the container, "If you put those on the table, these men can carry plates of food through, I'll make sure the coffee is in a pot so people can help themselves".

There was sudden banging heard from upstairs.

"Ah, the younger men of the house are awake, " Dave announced, "everyone, brace yourselves".

"Sure enough, all three boys came piling in to the kitchen, James followed while subconsciously assuming it was simply something that happened in this house.

"Since when has the smell of a cooked breakfast got you out of bed so fast?" Gwen asked. "I wouldn't know about you, James, but these two won't emerge from their pit for anything, if this is the secret, I'll do it every morning!"

"It does smell amazing, doesn't it Mum?!" James said to his Mum.

"I hear you're a bit of a chef yourself James? Gwen asked, "It's all I can do to get these two to make anything other than a cake", "still, not complaining, I shall put everything on a large platter and you can all help yourselves. Shall I do scrambled egg?"

There was an almost instant vote of yes from everyone, Noah took control of the other two boys. "James, take this to the table, "James was handed a large pitcher of cold apple juice straight from the fridge. Todd was handed some plastic tumblers to do the same and Noah made his way to the toaster, he made no delay in getting toast made with happy memories of the breakfast at Merlin's house, moments later the dining table was occupied and everyone was getting fed and watered, or indeed 'coffeed'. What's the plan today, Merlin?" Noah asked.

"Well, lad, yer Dad is taking me over to see Dan, I need to test a quick theory I've had which, if it works will get those of us travelling to the North pole, to our destination",

"Amazing, is everyone coming?"

Upon hearing that they were, while the Dads stayed behind in case anything needed doing that end, Noah punched the air with his fist with a victorious "Yes!" It was a shame his Dad and Ian weren't coming, but he was excited that James was.

Chapter Fourteen

After breakfast, it was time for Dave and Merlin to head over to Dan's cave, while it seemed odd that surely it would make sense for everyone to go at the same time, Merlin explained,

"Well, yes it would make sense for us all to head over now saving Dave two trips, however, we would still have to wait until midday for Bertha and Katy to arrive and it may end up being a wasted journey anyway because I've still got to check if my theory is correct because if it isn't I still need to get us all to the North pole, so, really, for my ow brain, let's stick to the original plan if that's alright with everyone".

Dave and Merlin jumped in Henrietta and set off. Meanwhile Kelly and James said goodbye to Ian, making absolutely sure he was okay with them going on the trip, which of course he said he was, he was very much looking forward to hearing all about it once they got back, the plan was, he and Dave would probably pop over to the pub in Oxford to help out if needed what with all the things that were going on over there, more hands would most likely be gratefully received. Once Dave and Merlin arrived at the cave, Merlin made his way back into the trees that they had been in before where they went through the large door with the others. Dave followed.

"Okay, Dave, what I need to do is head to both the games room where the boys were before and the observatory so you can either join me or go back to your man shed, purely your choice, I shouldn't be long but then I'll make my way back to Henrietta so we can get back, I will obviously pop my head in on Dandelion, obviously, just to check on him".

"Okay, Merlin, I'll stick with you, just in case you need my help with anything, seems silly to split up".

"As you wish, and thank you".

Merlin made the large door open as he had done before and the two men walked inside. The games room was first. Merlin had a question for the computer,

"Computer?"

"Yes Merlin, will you be playing today?"

"No not today, just a quick question"

"Certainly".

"When Noah, Todd and James entered here before, they mentioned that they met other children who spoke of meeting me themselves?"

"Correct, the other children are named Tim and Lucy, they are siblings, they entered via the same gateway you installed at their end, they had all thought of the same games and so I put them all together in the same environment. Was this okay or did you wish to change my settings?"

"No, no, that was absolutely fine, the 'other gateway', are you able to tell me where this is located?"

"Yes, it is by the rainbow quarter, which is located at the North Pole, Arctic circle".

"Interesting, and I installed this?"

"Yes, that is correct, the other you made the facility available for all the other children residing in the Rainbow quarter".

"Uh huh, now here's a question for you, does the Rainbow quarter exist within the same dimension and on the same plain as we are located here?"

"No, your suspicions are correct, the Rainbow quarter and it's surroundings exist outside of our time and space but I am able to connect to my counterpart, the other gateway, because we use the same magic, another interesting fact as I can tell you're curious, the other you is still you but exists also from a different time and space, you both share the same DNA code and are in fact one and the same person, just split somehow, almost like identical twins, I can research for more information to help give more details?"

"No, that's very good, if I wanted to would I and indeed others be able to pass through the other gateway and access the Rainbow quarter and it's surroundings via here if we wanted to?"

"Yes, I can help you with that"

"Lovely, expect me back here a little after midday local time, I will be bringing others with me, including Noah Todd and James again".

"Perfect, I will be ready".

"Dave this is perfect, no need to check the observatory now, all questions I needed answering have been, let's head back".

"No problem, "Dave answered, "that was a real brain teaser".

"Yes, "Merlin chuckled, "but I have a fairly airtight theory as to what has happened, most exciting!"

The two men made their way outside and back towards the car and cave. They stepped inside the cave to be greeted by Barry the badger.

"Good morning, gentlemen, what brings you here so early today?"

"Hello my fine fellow, "Merlin replied, "I needed to check on something and now I need a quick word with Dandelion, is he awake?"

"Yes I am, Master, "came a deep rumbling reply, "it's wonderful to see you".

"Oh, you too, can we step outside quickly?"

"Certainly".

Once outside, Dave said he would go and wait in the car while Merlin chatted with his dragon.

"So, a new adventure is afoot", Merlin began, "I am taking the young boys and their Mums to the North pole to try and solve a few mysteries. I have found a way to travel there so you mustn't worry about having to fly there unless you want to of course, you'd be most welcome, but I won't need to use you to carry anyone, it would be more like a holiday for you if you're interested".

"When are you leaving? And indeed coming back?"

"Leaving in the next few hours, waiting on Bertha and, Katy who you've not met yet, to join us. As for returning, I'm not sure how long we'll be there for, so I'm planning to return as close to the time we leave as possible, so you will literally not notice we've gone. I'm only really telling you in case the plan isn't possible, I don't want you to worry. If possible, if the owls could occasionally check on those left behind in Swindon, Marlborough and Oxford, but no pressure and as far as I'm concerned, we will return almost instantaneously".

"Okay I'll talk to the owls, please take the greatest care of yourself". Dan leant forward to put his head next to Merlin and was rewarded by the rub of the left ear he was wishing for.

"Thank you, you really are brilliant, Must go, got to return to Swindon to pick people up, we will return soon! Bye for now, my wonderful beast, my love to all the animals in the cave with you".

"Good bye, Master", Dan slowly backed himself in through the cave entrance, laying down and closing his eyes. Dave started up Henrietta and drove back to Swindon.It was still early when they got back, certainly enough time to pop back in the house and make sure everything had been remembered for the big trip. The boys were sat watching TV, the adults were still sat at the dining table, still making their way through the coffee. Dave and Merlin entered.

"Well?" Noah asked, "How's your theory looking, Merlin?"

"You'll be pleased to know I was bang on, I suggest we leave no later than eleven, give us time to get there, assess any potential issues etcetera. At half past ten, Gwen walked over to the boys, "right everyone, toilet check time, then into the car please". To Gwen's amazement, this worked, the three boys ran upstairs, the adults quickly tidied up the remains of the breakfast into the kitchen, everyone was in the car ready for eleven as per Merlin's suggestion, a quick drive back to the cave found Dan napping with his head resting on the ground outside the entrance, he was only snoozing though, so he was aware of the car arriving and lifted his head to welcome everyone. The three boys and Merlin were the first ones out of the car. Noah and Todd ran over to say hello. James was slightly apprehensive. As brave as he was, seeing a dragon for the first time was quite a surprise.

"It's okay, " said Todd, "This is Dan, if you rub his left ear like this, "he demonstrated, "you'll be best friends for life, he loves it, don't you, Dan". Dan agreed with a low satisfied rumble.

"Told you we'd be back soon", Merlin stated, "Just got to wait for the others now, I think I can hear a motorbike, so that may be Will with someone hanging on the back".

Merlin was correct again, Will drew up next to the car, climbed off his bike and helped Katy off. "Hi everyone, "Will began, "I've got to pop back, I left Bertie behind at my house as I can only get one passenger on the bike at a time, won't be long". Will jumped back on the bike and whizzed off leaving everyone waving. Noah was already giving Katy a hug, who in turn greeted everyone.

"Will came all the way to Oxford to come get me, isn't that sweet? Bertie has done really well finding him, I'm so happy for both of them, I'm not suggesting Sam isn't kind too, I'm sure he would have got me here if he had transport, hello Merlin, "she said hugging him too.

"Hello my dear, so glad you could make it, yes, Will is quite the excellent young man, clever, kind, I'm also happy that he and Bertha found each other, under quite extraordinary odds too, now, have you had breakfast? Most of us have, but if you're in need of a light bite, I have my magic hamper in the back of Dave's car still I believe".

"Oh I'm fine, Sam and I made a great breakfast in the pub kitchen earlier so I'm all good, but thank you, magic hamper?"

Merlin asked Dave to open up the back of the car and showed Katy the picnic hamper used on the previous trip with everyone, explained how it worked so she reached in and pulled out an apple, "I do have a weakness for a juicy apple I must admit, "she said. The three boys asked if they could have another go, with the excuse of stocking up on a few sugary snacks for the journey.

"Not too many, boys, thank you, "said Gwen, "you've not got bags or indeed big enough pockets and we're certainly not carrying things for you".

"Don't worry, "Merlin stepped in, "I'm sure we can conjure up things on our journey if needed, help yourselves, " he chuckled. The boys wasted no time pulling chocolate, and other sugary things out of the hamper such as doughnuts, cupcakes, biscuits but quickly realised they'd have to put most of it back for another time.After what felt like no time at all, Will's motorbike could be heard again. Moments later Will came into view with Bertha hanging on tightly behind. Once again, Will climbed off the bike and helped his passenger do the same. This time it was Todd who felt compelled to step forward to be the first to get a hug from Bertha.

"Hello you, "she looked at Katy and mouthed, "so sweet", afterwards, Bertha and Katy had a hug too. "William got you here okay then?"

"Yes, perfectly, I'd never been on the back of a motorbike before, I think I'd secretly always wanted to though".

"I know what you mean, although it wasn't until Dad and I travelled to the future or as you know it, 'now', that I even knew such a thing existed. The fastest thing I'd ever travelled on was a dragon, talking of which, come with me, you need to meet Dan", Bertha grabbed Katy's hand and pulled her toward the cave entrance, she called Dan's name from the entrance, and suddenly Dan's head emerged from the cave. Bertha threw her arms around his neck, "hello lovely, meet Katy, Katy this is Dan, Dad's dragon, isn't he incredible? Dan, Katy is my great-grandmother, long story! Have you met everyone else?" Bertha didn't really want the answer, she decided to name everyone for him regardless and do introductions.

"It's so amazing that all of this should even exist all because of my amazing and famous grandson, "Katy said with a single tear forming in her eye and smiling at Merlin with an overwhelming feeling of pride.

Merlin broke a silence with, "no time quite like the present, those travelling with me, please form an orderly queue".

"Hang on, Merlin, "said Will, " I need to rig you up with a few bits, also, if I can quickly just take your phone, oh and Bertie's, if that's ok. Also, Bertie, you're less likely to lose this, it's just a little bit of tech that can be clipped to your clothing somewhere, or even if you wanted to you could wear it in your hair?It has a few colourful blinky lights on it so should satisfy your love of shiny/pretty things. Right just setting your phones to share your location with me, but if like I suspect there's no mobile signal where you're going the shiny tech should do the job, I've not had opportunity to test it so, fingers crossed, eh".

"Well, if it doesn't you know that I'll be safe with Dad, it's not like you've got other incredible technology to work before is it, "Bertha teased, winking warmly and squeezing his hand as she let him carefully pin the small piece of technology to her hair.

"Merlin, Will continued, "I'm going to increase my chances of tracking you both by putting an extra one of these in your hood" the two of them shook hands, "please take care of yourself and of course Bertie and Katy, I need you all to come back again,Katy, I'll be back at the pub helping Sam and attempting to track you all, so don't worry about him, we'll look out for eachother. See you all very soon".

Dave turned to Gwen, "look after yourself and the boys, expect anything with Merlin leading you all astray in the frozen North.

"I heard that", Merlin responded.

"I will check in with Chris and Zoe and update them both on everything although my current plan is to pop over to Oxford to see if they can make use of me there, Ian's coming with too, we'll look after eachother too, Kelly, don't worry, all will be fine". There was a sudden car horn heard as a small green car arrived.

"Auntie Zoe!" Todd called out. Zoe stepped out the car.

"Auntie?" Kelly asked.

"Not exactly, more like distant cousin in reality, " Gwen remarked, This is Will's Mum, Zoe this is Dave's cousin, Kelly, More introductions had to happen before Merlin had any hope of pressing on.

"My fault, "said Will, "I filled Mum in on everything before I left for Oxford earlier",

"Oh absolutely, so as you can imagine, I couldn't just sit at home waiting for the next time Will decided to drag himself home again, I simply had to find out everything for myself, never was one for missing out"

Gwen quickly gave a full summary and then suggested that Zoe join them, "more the merrier, Zo, an extra adult to keep eye on the kids etcetera".

"Oh I'm not sure, what about Chris?"

"Well Dave and Kelly's Ian aren't coming, neither is Will so all the men will have eachother, Dave did say he was going to pop over to yours at some point anyway".

"Oh, well, I suppose, I wouldn't be one too many would I?"

"Of course not"said Gwen, Bertha and Merlin at the same time.

"What about my car though? I can't just leave it here".

"There's every chance we'll be returning to this exact location if that helps? Merlin commented.

"Or…" Dave stepped forward, "I reckon we could get Will's bike in the back of Henrietta, Ian gets in with me, Will drives your car and the three of us head back to yours then your car is at home, Will has his bike, Ian and I have Henrietta. Job done".

"Sold!" said Will.

"Be careful with my lovely little car, young man!" Zoe demanded.

"Yes of course, Mum", Will went to open the car door when Bertha suddenly stepped forward, "Erm, excuse me, William, where is my goodbye?" The women all looked at each other with a raised eyebrow as if to say, "oh dear, he's in trouble".

"Oh no, " said Todd.

"What is it? "asked James.

"\They're going to kiss aren't they" Todd remarked with a scrunched up disgusted face.

"Yup, I'm afraid so, "Noah said.

"Sorry my love, "said Will putting his hands around her waist and pulling her toward him, they did indeed kiss although quickly to save embarrassment followed by Bertha throwing her arms around him, "Bye bye, my William, I love you, "she whispered in his ear, see you soon.

Will leaned close and whispered "Love you too, it won't be soon enough" in her ear.

"Are you done?" Todd said impatiently.

"Todd!" Gwen barked, "leave them be, it's sweet, you'll understand when you're older".

Bertha moved over to Todd and gave him a quick hug, "It's okay, just gonna miss him is all, not even completely sure why really".

"Thanks, " said Will.

"Right, "said Merlin, "if we're all done, those of you coming with, follow me over to the trees, again for some of you. Gentlemen, "he said addressing Dave, Ian and Will, "keep an eye on us if you wish, look out for messages, signals, even unobvious ones, I can get quite inventive when I need to, best wishes to all, we will all celebrate our mutual successes upon our return".

Will opened the door of his Mum's car, again and stood waving as did Dave and Ian from Henrietta until the travelling company had disappeared from view into the trees. A bright light came from the trees from where Merlin opened the large door again. Dave then remembered and shouted "Goodbye Dan, see you again soon!" toward the cave.

A low voice rumbled, "Farewell everyone" and then there was quiet, the two cars left and headed for the middle of Marlborough, the travelling company stepped inside the large door in the trees to find themselves, for most, once again, in a large hallway with arches going down both sides stretching out into the distance, Each archway had a door as before.

"Okay everyone, "Merlin announced, "you boys in particular, we must make our way to the games room, but be careful not to enter without me, please, we're going to do things a little differently this time". The boys all ran off but knew to just find the door and wait outside for the others to catch up. They decided to sit on the familiar bench directly outside the door. James then reached into the hood he just happened to have on his top and pulled out a packet of wagon wheels, a chocolate treat that he was particularly fond of and proceeded to share them with Noah and Todd, "I managed to stow these away from the hamper earlier, if you haven't tried them before they're really nice!"

"James you're a genius, "Noah declared, " thank you.

"Yes, thank you, " Todd followed up with, "this'll show Mummy, then said in a mock impersonation of Gwen "you don't have pockets and we're not carrying it all for you!"

"Quick, they're almost here", said Noah, parking three quarters of his remaining wagon wheel in his mouth. The other two followed his example and all stuffed their empty wrappers into a nearby bin, a nice detail which came as part of the illusion that this building was basically a museum.

"What are you boys up to?" Gwen asked as she approached, "you all look guilty".

The boys obviously denied anything and everything but unconvincingly giggled too. Merlin meanwhile turned his attention to the door under the sign reading Games room. "Ok, assorted ladies and young men, when we enter, please try not to touch anything, interact with anything, allow me to talk with the computer assistant, you boys know what I'm talking about", all three boys nodded while still trying to deal with the wagon wheels they hadn't quite consumed yet. "Okay, let's go in."

Merlin entered first and as before the assembled group were greeted by a large screen monitor with a computer generated voice asking them to state their names. Merlin cleared his throat, "Hello again computer, I'm back as previously declared. I have with me, these fine young fellows whom you will no doubt recognise, Noah, Todd and James. Computer for now please don't analyse their preferences, I need to take control of this particular expedition".

"Understood, Merlin, settings have been altered but can be restored to their original state by you at any time", said the computer, "please continue to add names".

"Ah yes, these ladies are, in no particular order,, Katy, my Grandmother, Bertha, my daughter, Gwen my descendant and Zoe another descendant".

"Thank you, I have a question for....Zoe, are you sure that is your name? I have recently registered another person who bears a striking resemblance to yourself and matches certain key points in your DNA".

"Oh, well my name has always been Zoe and I have no reason to believe it will ever change, "came the reply.

"Computer, "Merlin interrupted, "does this person who closely resembles Zoe still reside on the other side of your counterpart gateway?"

"She does" the computer replied.

"Excellent, I have a theory of who she is, but don't tell me any more, I want to find out for myself and have it be a surprise for everyone else".

"How very intriguing, "Zoe commented, "I do love a mystery".

"Probably another relative we haven't met yet" Todd said in another of his uniquely intuitive moments, "just like when Mum met Merlin's wife back in 13th century Tintagel and they looked just like each other, it'll be something like that again I reckon".

"Oh we went to Tintagel once, it wasn't the 13th century, it was just a spur of the moment visit about twenty years ago, these days it's a heritage site and tourist attraction" said Kelly.

Gwen sidled up to Kelly to say "Careful you're in danger of talking like you completely believe in everything that's being said without question, oh I'm so happy you're on board".

Once Gwen had finished squeezing all the air out of Kelly with one of her famous full on hugs, she replied, "well, in for a penny, in for a pound as they say I suppose I'm just trying to get in to the spirit of it all, I still reserve the right to be unamazed if some aspects of all of this is no more real than any other incredible story. Don't get me wrong, I want all of it to be true and real because it's wonderful, all of it".

Merlin stepped forward, "well, with that in mind, computer, could you kindly recreate the last setting the boys had where they met the other children please?"

Chapter Fifteen

"**Y**es certainly, if you would all care to walk through the door behind my monitor like before, you'll be back where you were before". They all stepped through, Merlin first then the three boys then the four women, and sure enough it was just as the boys remembered it. A long log cabin, with views of snow covered landscapes outside.

"Computer?" Merlin began to ask, "is it as cold outside as it looks, bearing in mind we are now in the arctic circle, if so could you please provide warm clothing such as coats, gloves and scarves for all?"

"Certainly, these can be found inside the benches along the wall, simply lift the seats" came the answer. James was the first to notice that the wall above the seats had everyone's names on little plaques so everyone found their name, lifted the seat of the bench and reached inside for their clothing. While getting on their jackets and warm things another door opened through which appeared a small boy.

"Tim!" shouted James, "you're back!"

"So are you" Tim chuckled, "great to see you, and you Noah, and you Todd, and Merlin!" he exclaimed, throwing his arms around Merlin's waist, "we weren't sure if you were ever coming back, everyone will be overjoyed to see you, are you staying longer this time? Why did you come this way? We assumed you'd use the portal again, it's still there, the lost boys have been using it constantly"

"The lost boys?" asked Noah, "as in Peter Pan's lost boys?"

"Yes that's them, always in search of adventure"

"Tim, can I ask, where's Lucy?" Todd asked.

"Oh she's also here somewhere, playing with some of her friends, no idea where, you could always talk to her on the walkie-talkie things, or hopefully if you're all sticking around long enough this time, you'll see each other in person later".

"Sorry to pose another question to you, Tim, but can I be bold and ask you your full name? Just to satisfy a hunch of mine".

"Oh, Merlin, you are funny, as I said the last time you asked me that, everyone calls me Tiny Tim, actual name, Tim Cratchit. Yes I'm tiny but may I add, I'm nearly 4ft tall, plus which I'm only seven years old, nearly eight, so still plenty of time to grow Dad always said".

"Oh of course you are, "Merlin chuckled, clapping his hands together, "of course, Tim and Lucy, two of the Cratchit children, ah, of course, that would mean, " he paused in thought, "you say the lost boys are here too? Everyone, if you'll excuse me for a short while, I need to go to the observatory, but I will return, I'm sure you'll all be okay, "Computer?"

"Yes, Merlin" the computer voice replied, "How can I assist you?"

"I need to exit the games room just for a brief moment but will return, please help everyone here with whatever they need. I have faith in you that you can help everyone while still not adhering to their subconscious wants and preferences. Remember everyone, anything you need, any questions, the computer is designed to be your assistant, use it, my advice is don't wander off too far but don't worry, I will find you!" he smiled at everyone in turn, then said, "computer, exit!" at which point he simply vanished and reappeared back outside in the main hall of arches and doors, just as the three boys had done during their last visit. He made his way to the observatory up the staircase that had been used before. "Right," he started to mumble to himself, "according to google there is no phone reception to speak of at the North pole because there isn't enough population to justify it, so we'll just have to create our own, oh Will you're going to be so proud of me lad, I'll prove to you I'm not just an old beard, I can keep up with modern technology, just see if I don't, now, google said something about satellite phones which seemed to be the answer, let's find out, now, where did he pin that tracker? I'm thinking a little ancient magic just to give a little extra pep, it's good to be doing old magic again". A fizz, a bang and a few sparks later and Merlin had done everything he could think to do. So, with that, he went back downstairs and across to the games room.

"Hello again, computer, only me".

"Greetings again, Merlin, welcome back, that was quick!, The others are still where you left them, I can tell they're eager to investigate further but I haven't encouraged this, feel free to go through".

"Lovely, thank you for keeping an eye on them, very much appreciated".

"Most welcome, please send my regards to all the others when you meet them".

"Will do".

Merlin made his way through the door they used before and found everyone still accounted for, ready and waiting for his return.

"Welcome back, Merlin, "Noah said, "everything okay?"

"Yes, indeed, just a few little magic things I needed to take care of, now, if anyone has their mobile phones and wishes to send any last messages to loved ones, I would suggest now is the time, once we go through the next part of this, I can't guarantee you'll have any signal or way of contacting anyone". Gwen sent a quick message to Dave to assure him everyone was okay and everything was going well, nothing to report just yet. Kelly sent a similar message to Ian while Bertha sent

---

---- Hello William, just to say, so far so good, we've made it so far to a log cabin in the middle of somewhere, feels like nowhere, very pretty though with all the snow. I hope you're taking care of yourself, everyone here is well and okay, missing you already xx

---

Will replied as quickly as he could,

Hi Bertie. All is good here, we arrived back at home not that long ago, tell Mum her car is okay as promised. Dad's fine too, we've introduced him and Ian to each other already obviously. We're popping to Oxford soon, miss you too. According to tracking you literally disappeared for a mere second and reappeared and look to still be in the middle of the arctic circle. Impressive! It suggests Merlin's plan is working, please look after yourself, love you, W xx

---

    Katy also sent a message to Sam of course but was more reminding him of things that needed doing at the pub than anything too romantic, but she did assure him that Will had got her to the rendezvous point okay and their trip was now well underway. There was no response, because he had left his phone under the bar, this was a normal everyday occurrence so Katy wasn't worried, no doubt he would discover the message later, panic and do his best to reply with something loving, apologetic and they would both laugh about it. Merlin spoke once more, "Computer, we are ready to see the other gateway please".

    "Certainly, Merlin, please wait while the visual element finishes rendering before stepping through" came the reply.

    "Understood, young Tim, might I suggest that you lead the way as we have no idea what to expect on the other side of this, while I know an alternative me has been there before and everything the computer has assessed about me suggests the Merlin you met before is definitely me as well, I can assure you this is my first visit, it's complicated, I'm not completely sure I understand it myself, but I'm determined to find out and figure where the other me has gone and indeed how we both exist simultaneously, particularly if we are indeed both the same person.Okay everyone, listen to Tim, he is going to know the place we end up in next far better than we do, once we are through, we will have left the games room environment, in other words we are entering a real world environment, so common sense is key, Tim, after you young man".

    Tim turned into what could have easily been mistaken as the world's first child travel guide. "Okay everyone if you'd like to follow me, we are stepping in to what we call the holding area, if you could make sure you stay close enough to be able to hear me, ladies and gentlemen, it is my honour to welcome you all to the Rainbow quarter, everything here is labelled with accompanying signs to ensure you know where you are at all times, every coloured shape you see around you is a zone, we have many different rooms for all different purposes, we have social spaces, places to get food and drink, if you would care to follow me, you can get a better idea of how big this place is from the outside. "Tim encouraged everyone to follow him out into the cold."I hope you're all properly wrapped up and warm, we get good weather here but it is the North pole so the average temperature during the day tends to be anywhere between zero and minus forty degrees celsius depending which season we're in, we are currently in Winter so yes, it's very cold. So let's stand out the front of this complex. You will notice it is made up of many different shaped blocks or pods in a variety of colours. Each child has their own pod which has access to all the other facilities so you have quick access to what you need including your friends, you will always find it easy to find your pod again, not only by location but because your personal pod shines in your own personal favourite colour, if you look up to the left you will see our portal which we are allowed to use to help us transport to anywhere in the world, lovingly installed by Merlin who apparently has his own portal installed at his home".

"Look Todd, "said Noah, "it's exactly the same as Alice's looking glass again".

"Oh yeah, "Todd replied, "This whole place has you written all over it, Merlin".

"I agree, I never realised more than one of those looking glasses existed, I had my suspicions, but only because Lewis Carroll never divulged where he got his from, it was only on closer inspection that I realised it had magical properties. Tim, tell me more about the geography of this place".

"Well, okay, we don't usually stray far from here just because we have everything we need, but just over there is the frozen lake which is always frozen, that's how it got its name, just North of us is called rock bridge, there is water here which doesn't always freeze but forms the top of the river Telmar".

"Wait, I know that name, could it possibly be?Those trees over there, "said Merlin pointing East, "would they by some bizarre coincidence be known as the Shuddering wood?"

"Yes, you know it, you are Merlin, you have the same excited look in your eyes as you did the last time you discovered where you are, what else can you remember?"

"At the Northernmost point of the shuddering woods is where you will find Father Christmas? Yes, I know this place very well, in the far North is the witch's castle, good lord, it's all coming back, but what could cause such a coincidence that I should end up back here, a place so familiar to me and yet perfectly described by someone so unconnected to me in his series of books? It makes no sense, Tim, you do all realise where we are?" Everyone looked blankly at Merlin except for Noah who had an inkling he knew something, an answer maybe."Go on, Noah, tell us, you know don't you"

"No I don't, "Noah protested.

"I could give you a few clues to reassure you and help give your confidence that you're on the right track?"

"Ok?"

"Well, head east and you come to the witch's camp, further east again, you come to a certain stone table and beyond that the Cair Paravel"

"And on to the East Sea?"

"You got it, lad, can you name the island in the east sea?"

"Galma?"

"Bang on, lad, you've got all the evidence you need, now tell us where we are?"

"But we can't be"

"Why ever not?"

"Everyone, if I'm wrong I'm gonna look like an idiot, but, 'Welcome to Narnia!' But, Merlin, how did Jack know about this place or did he create it and we found it?"

"I don't have an answer for that yet, but I know a man who will, troops, follow me, it's time to find Father Christmas! North East from here I believe"

"Come on everyone, " Tim announced, "I'll show you the way, it doesn't take long.

"Quick question", Todd began, "Tim, if this really is Narnia, where is the wardrobe?"

"Well, the easiest and safest way to do it is to make your way anti-clockwise around the perimeter of the Western woods which are just over the other side of the frozen lake, follow it all round you will come to the beaver dam, a bit further round, you'd find the house of one Mr Tumnus, turn round and you would see a lamppost, look beyond the lamppost to the South and there will be the wardrobe, that's where it was the last time anyone was asked"

"And what about Aslan?" Noah asked, "Aslan's camp, "Tim answered "is East from here beyond the witch's camp and the fords of Beruna, North of the stone table".

"Let's press on, we must get to Father Christmas if we can" said Merlin.

"Not far, this way" Tim continued. They walked for about 20 minutes before a clearing appeared, and what they found was another log cabin but this one was covered in coloured lights, including around the decking at the front, as if it didn't look quite festive and inviting enough, smoke could be seen coming out of a chimney on the roof by way of a large open fire glowing in one of the windows.

"This looks like the place, I'll knock on the front door shall I?" Merlin suggested.

"Good idea, Merlin, "Gwen spoke up", quite cold out here, looks cosy in there though doesn't it!"She turned to the other women, "don't know about you girls, but I'm glad the log cabin thing provided warm boots, I was wearing completely the wrong things on my feet, I'd have been in a bit of bother there I reckon!"

"Bertie and I are hoping we might get to hold on to ours, "Katy admitted, "only, they're not only warm, they're really comfy and they're really quite fashionable, luckily Bertie and I have the same size feet, we compared them side by side which means we can swap them sometimes".

"That's a great idea, what size are you Gwen?" Zoe asked.

"Oh, I'm nearer the hobbit, me, size 9, Zo".

"Wow, okay, forget that then, "they all laughed at the idea. Meanwhile Merlin wasn't standing around listening to women chat, he had approached the door and was currently banging the large door with his closed fist. A voice, a strangely familiar one was suddenly heard, on it's way to answer the door, "on my way, bear with me".

Chapter Sixteen

"The large door was green on the outside, red on the inside and had a large wreath hung on the outside made of things presumably found on the ground in the woods, things of nature so twigs, different colour leaves, a sleeping squirrel, definitely just sleeping, Merlin poked it to make sure. The voice that was heard belonged to a woman who opened the door slowly as if peeking around it. She was of slim build with raven black hair and piercing blue eyes. Any silence was broken by Todd who shouted "Auntie Zoe, it's you!"

"Oh my!" Zoe responded when she saw the woman, "I think you must be right, Todd, because even I can see the resemblance".

"Are you okay, Bertie?" Katy asked.

Bertha had tears forming in her eyes, "yes, I'm ok", she walked over toward the woman in the doorway, "If I'm wrong about this, it will sound so weird and stupid so I apologise in advance, but, "

"Hello Bertha my beautiful niece, yes it's me".

"Auntie Gan!" arms were thrown around each other, "what are you doing here?"

"Well, that was going to be my question, but knowing your Father I suppose it was inevitable. I live here my lovely. Hello, Merlin, you haven't changed a bit, how are you?" Merlin and his sister hugged each other tightly.

"So good to see you, so glad I found you. I guessed you'd be here, but I wasn't 100% sure, I've gone through a lot of travelling, meeting folk and guessing, putting two and two together and getting four, more times than incorrect answers thankfully. Now my next assumption leads me to an obvious question, where's the big man?"

"Hang on, "his sister smiled, she turned back into the doorway and shouted, "NICK! Visitor!"

"Glad you're both still, well, you know"

"Alive?"

"Well, yes, but I'm sure we would have heard something, if the worst had happened".

"You make a habit of talking to dead people do you, Merlin?"

"Well, as it happens, it's become quite the regular thing lately, but we'll get to that later". The sound of heavy footsteps and a deep rumbling, not like Dan's of course, this was from an old aged human who was less than happy about having to get up from his afternoon nap.

"Who is it dear?" came the booming voice.

"Oh you'll see, there's more than one actually, all outside." was the reply.

"Oh! Ominous". The large man threw open the door to see Merlin standing before him looking quite small and old but the beard was unmistakable as was his typical hooded cloak though he had wisely adopted a scarf back at the games room. "Merlin? Goodness me, well I didn't expect that, Come here, brother". The large man picked Merlin up and gave him a full on bear hug much to the amusement of everyone watching. It was like watching a normal size human pick up a scrawny blue parrot and hugging it tightly. The noise coming from Merlin was similar to a parrot being crushed too, lots of squawking and occasionally enough air to say something like, "put me down this instant you silly great bear".

"Right!" The large man thundered, "everyone inside, it's as cold as a picnic on the moon out here, I've got a large log fire going indoors, everyone welcome, let's get in before things start freezing and dropping off shall we?

Nobody thought this was a bad idea and all filed into the cabin to find what could only be described as the sort of grotto you might see at a garden centre around Christmas, where children are invited in to 'meet santa himself'.

"Okay, Merlin started, "rubbing his hands together as close to the flames of the roaring fire as he'd dare, "introductions. "So, ladies and children, you would be right in thinking this gentleman here is indeed Father Christmas himself, he is also one of my oldest friends, when we met he was known as Nicholas, though I expect some of you have already jumped ahead of me and worked out what he is now better known as, "Old Saint Nick".

"Less of the old, Merlin, you're no spring chicken yourself, ya know".

"True, no offence, old friend, and this lady here, is my wonderful sister, known affectionately to Bertha as Auntie Gan, her full name being Ganieda,she is also Nick's wife. At least I automatically assume that is still the case?"

"Yes of course it is. And for the record I've never really liked my name if I'm being honest, but you get used to these things I suppose"

"Excuse me, " Noah interrupted cautiously "I have an idea".

"How lovely, Noah, what's your idea?"

"Well, two things actually, Firstly, how do you know my name?

"Well, that's Santa's doing to be fair, he knows by sight the name of every child that exists, more or less anyway and some of that skill has rubbed off on me over the years, I'm thinking the young man next to you is your brother Todd and you, "she said looking at James, "are their cousin, James".

Todd and James looked at eachother and mouthed the word "wow", meanwhile Noah who was unimpressed and suspected information about them had been passed on to her somehow, or magic, but whatever it was, he was going to figure it out. He continued, "My other thought was that if you don't like your name, would you be okay if we called you Mrs Claus?"

"Oh, I quite like that, yes I agree, Mrs Claus, Bertha you may call me whatever you feel comfortable with, I will always be Auntie Gan if that's what you need".

"Of course, you can all call me what you like given I've been given a whole variety of names over the years from children all over the world so I'm used to it" Santa exclaimed. At this point, Noah inevitably let his guard down because of his now overwhelming need to give 'Mrs Claus' a hug.

"Bring it in, Noah, "she said, "I can see you, I'm definitely a hugger, so is Santa when he feels he has to be, though he'll never admit to it".

"Well he hugged the very life out of me just outside", Merlin said, "However, moving on, yes, you're right about the names of the boys, now this is where it gets complicated, First we have Noah and Todd's mum, Gwen",

"Looks exactly the same as your Gwendolyn, Merlin, practically the same name, what's that about?" Santa chuckled.

"Well you'll have to bear with me on this because I admit it does sound somewhat fantastical even to me, however this charming lady is a descendant of mine, by around 800 years, and indeed after her is young Noah and Todd".

"Okay", said his sister calmly.

"And the one who could pass for Gan under any interrogation?" Santa chuckled again.

"Another descendant called Zoe, who is not only of similar age but I discovered they ended up living quite close to one another in the future, coincidence or not, it's quite extraordinary. And so, Bertha you know, so that's her explained, erm, the other young lady is Kathryn but prefers Katy, "

"Oh I like that name, far nicer than mine, and where do you fit into this fascinating mix, Katy?"

Katy stepped forward, "hello Mrs Claus, I'm a close friend of Bertie's, "

"Oh and she calls Bertha, Bertie isn't that lovely, I love that so much, now tell me, why did our mother completely bypass all the pretty girl names like Katy and Zoe and Bertie and somehow arrive at Ganieda?

"There's one other thing you should know, "Merlin began, "there is one other significant way that Katy, as you phrased it 'fits in the mix'.

"Oh, how exciting, another descendant?"

"No, not quite, well, seven of us here are actually descended from her, you and I included, Katy is in fact our Grandmother, our Mother's Mother to be exact, Bertha's Great Grandmother, you get the idea".

"But how?" Mrs Claus stuttered.

"Well, I always was one to pop off visiting the future because as far as I could deduce, it was far safer than endangering our existence by going into the past, obviously, "Merlin replied.

"Obviously, "came the counter-reply heavily soaked in sarcasm and rolling eyes. "Much like when you would swan off looking for knights, I was never overly sure why".

"The King, Gan, don't you remember? He commissioned me to find significant people across time to join the round table, and more importantly, had I not, I never would have met Gwen's husband Dave, who incidentally is cousin to Kelly here who until now I have neglected to introduce, sorry Kelly, very remiss of me, and, on a unique adventure Dave, Gwen and their two boys along with a smattering of others joined me back to Tintagel of the past to help me rescue Gwendolyn (long story, I have it written down) and meanwhile, Bertha met her brilliant young gentleman friend, William or Will as he prefers, I haven't quite figured out why young people started to shorten their names, I've known plenty of Williams and Kathryns, perfectly happy with their names, still, never mind, I think the point I'm trying to get across is, that, life has a way of sorting itself out and I can't help thinking that some things are meant to be".

"That's not quite the Merlin I remember", Gan replied.

"Talking of which, I'm led to believe I was here recently? A few of people seem to think so anyway".

"Yes, you were here very recently, don't you remember? You had the Rainbow quarter created".

"Did I indeed? Interesting! According to the AI analysis back inside another creation of mine, the Merlin that was here was absolutely me, but I assure you it wasn't. Seems the other Merlin's DNA is absolutely identical to mine, I am reasonably sure I have never been here before, or at least not recently, the only thing that resembles some sort of evidence to support the idea is this letter which I received from myself very recently". He retrieved the letter which he had carried in his pocket, he handed it to his sister, "of course I had a job figuring out details like where it had been sent from, luckily young Todd figured it out, it was obvious to him that it must have come from here because of all the glitter that came with it which always seems to replenish itself each time the letter is put back in the envelope and then reopened".

"Ah yes, I'm glad the post elves still include the glitter, that's a nice touch we thought, and of course the fact that it keeps re-appearing, another brilliant touch by one of our inventor elves, very clever, because before, the glitter would simply disappear in the real world, a safety measure introduced a long time ago, because we need to protect the idea that this place does actually exists, we try to maintain the magic at all times, which is why, you will now notice, if you look at the letter again, you can see that it is letter-headed complete with address, co-ordinates, and has the official Santa Claus stamp on it, it's old stock so, rather than waste it we still encourage it's use, we know it's perfectly safe and will simply disappear once it leaves this area" Gan/Mrs Claus explained.

"But why would it all disappear?" Merlin asked.

"Well because we exist on a different plane of existence of course, I'm amazed you didn't realise that, the other you knew about it, but I think this version of you is still catching up, perhaps I need to unload as much information as I can and get you up to date".

"It's a good idea, I can help with questions, I have many".

"So does Noah I think, I can tell ya know", she said with her eyes twinkling, "what would you like to know?"

Noah stepped forward to say "Todd, James and I were wondering if you and Santa kept any pets?"

"Ah, you'll be thinking of the reindeer I assume? Well we have ten of those, it was just nine for a very long time but then one day we happened upon a very old reindeer living and wandering alone over in Ettinsmoor, just East of the Witch's castle. Her name is Agnes. They all live over at the Rainbow quarter. With the children and assorted elves whose job it is to take care of them, you can pop over and meet them later if you wish"

"I'll take them, "said Tim who was still there with them but had kept himself to himself in the corner of a window, looking out at the amazing view of the snow covered trees".

"Thank you, Tim, I imagine we will all go across at some point".

"What about the squirrel on the front door?" asked Todd.

"Oh that little darling is Freya, we've been known to leave the wreath hung on the day after the season for a while, we haven't the heart to take it away from her, it's like we're moving her home, sweet thing. I'm afraid we don't have any pets like you might consider pets like cats or dogs, we get the occasional wolf wandering up to the cabin, then there's Betty. She's a Yeti, but she usually keeps herself to herself in the woods, she can be very useful for lifting logs and other heavy lifting, very helpful".

"Betty the Yeti?" Todd asked, sniggering.

"Oh yes, of course there's Una, she's a unicorn, haven't seen her for a while, I suspect she's over at the Rainbow quarter too. Very good friends with Agnes, Agnes can't see a lot these days so Una plays the part of her eyes, stops her walking into things, solid things".

Nick/Santa stood up. "Merlin, do you really not remember this place, not necessarily this cabin, I mean the land around here, is none of it familiar to you?"

"Well, I did gradually fall in where I was once we were in the shuddering woods, but I don't understand how I knew it, if the other me that has been here recently wasn't in fact me but somehow was and I have no recollection of being here pretty much ever let alone recently, can only mean I was either here a long time ago or at some point in the future (not the first time that's happened), or I'm going senile in my old age, again we're not on unfamiliar territory with that".

"Okay, there are definitely things missing in your knowledge, Merlin. Do you remember my Grandfather?"

"Yes I think so, Looked like you but with a far bigger beard".

"That's the chap, well, as you may or may not remember he was the original 'Saint Nick' he was the one that started it all including securing this location as a sort of central hub where children across space and time could have somewhere to call home and in order to do that, he realised he had to have a location where space and multi-dimensions could exist. As he got older, much older, he passed the mantle to my Father, Also called Nick or Nicholas, same beard, bigger belly, and so the tradition continues".

At this point Mrs Claus spotted Noah, Todd, James and by now Tim all sat on a couple of large bean bags in front of the fire listening to Santa's history lesson, she made the very wise decision to make several large mugs of warm, creamy hot chocolate with whipped cream on top, included was a single flake chocolate bar on the accompanying saucer. She put them on a tray and placed it in front of them on a foot-stall. Each mug also had each boy's name on it so they knew which one was who's. Upon seeing the eyes of all the adults light up, including Merlin and Santa, she prepared the same for them too.

Santa continued, "Thanks love, a favourite of mine this is. Where was I? Ah yes, Dad. So we spent a lot of our family time here, then one day in the (real-world) year 450, word reached my Father that a very very important child and his sister had arrived in the village of Tintagel, Cornwall, England from the year (real-world) 2085, one thousand six hundred and thirty five years in the future. Well, without thinking twice, he grabbed me, we jumped in the sleigh and set off on a rescue mission. We raced as fast as we could and landed just outside the village so as to not attract too much attention. We set about searching the village, asking people if they had seen any children, obviously Dad did the asking, it might have seemed odd for a child to be asking if children had been seen. Eventually we found you both hiding in an inn, and after making sure you were okay, fed and watered, you joined us in the sleigh and came home with us. You were the first children to be given shelter here all those years ago. Of course by the late 12th century(real-world time) we were all adults and you decided you wanted to return to the real-world and pick up where you left off. You felt you needed to try and find out about your past in the future and why you ended up in Tintagel. We visited when we could, I would bother Dad all the time to do so because I wanted to see Gan of course and after time she and I fell in love and decided to return here, not very long after you married Gwendolyn and of course, young Bertha was born, we returned here to help Dad who was incredibly old even then. My Grandfather was a spirit by that time so he took less to look after. We always meant to return for a visit but life became incredibly busy especially after Dad became a spirit too, I then took up the mantle of Santa and we've been here ever since. We never did have children of our own so we've simply carried on, thankfully we all seem to be blessed with very good longevity but we don't take that for granted, we have many things we want to accomplish and that need doing before we realise it's too late".

Chapter Seventeen

"So, I have questions," Merlin began, "obviously. Why do children come here? From what I can make out the Rainbow quarter is Idyllic providing it's inhabitants with everything they could want or need, correct?"

"Quite so," Santa confirmed.

"But where have they come from, I'm trying to understand their place here, their reason for being etcetera".

"Ok, let's take it back to basics. When my Grandfather was appointed the patron saint of Children, he took his appointed role very seriously and realised it's not just about bringing joy to their lives, but in many ways more about their protection and well being and so a place was created to serve that very purpose. Each child has a different story just as you both did when you arrived in Tintagel all those years ago. You had nowhere to turn and as I said earlier, you, Merlin in particular, were identified as particularly important, though it wasn't discovered in what way until much later".

"And the other children? I mean Tiny Tim here, until recently, only existed within the confines of fiction".

"So yes, the provision for children was put in place for children from everywhere, across the universe and indeed time, so some children here were never born, or never lived long enough to reach adulthood, some were orphans, some are characters from literature who, through no fault of their own, became lost in terms of their identity and where they belonged".

"That's what you said, isn't it Tim?" Todd asked out loud.

"Yes that's right, well you asked about the Rainbow quarter so I saw no harm in telling you as exactly as I could, how I understand it".

"Very good, young Tim, " Santa praised, "I suggest a tour of the Rainbow quarter for your three friends after we've finished here" he twinkled.

"Are you telling me, "Merlin interrupted, "that a significant number of children here are in fact the spirits of children who didn't survive either in the real world or in fiction, and that the spirits of others roam here too like you Father and Grandfather?"

"Precisely, Merlin", Santa replied, parking the last piece of chocolate flake into his mouth".

"But to my memory, Tiny Tim survived by the end of the book, Ebeneezer Scrooge was helped to see the error of his ways by three spirits and he then used his fortune for good, he helped Tim get better, this was the happily ever after timeline, however in the original timeline that the book starts with, Scrooge was a horrible old miser who made Tim's father Bob work all the hours available to him and didn't help. So I'm afraid Tim died. Scrooge was shown this outcome by the ghost of Christmas future which was partly responsible for Scrooge's change of heart, but because Tim died before the change of timeline, he ended up here where he has managed to achieve his own happily ever after, another success story for my Grandfather's legacy, now before you ask, Tim's sister Lucy has a different story because though she didn't die in the book, her own story was cut short by not having a definitive future written for her and so she became an example of a lost child, plus the bond between her and her brother was so strong, that arriving here was inevitable, if I'm completely honest, I don't always understand it one hundred percent myself. I simply accept it. Plenty of room for all"

"Here's a thought for you, do you suppose the other me which you refer to, was in fact a spirit? Either the me further along my own timeline or, like I suspect a bi-product from a near-death experience, something which I discussed with Nostradamus at length. The theory being, at some point I had a near-death experience, possibly when flying back from Southern France, from fogged memory maybe to do with the aeroplane that we nearly collided with, then I as flesh and blood me assumed we had survived and carried on, in this case to Chiseldon in Wiltshire. But then perhaps my jilted spirit which we will assume can both exist both inside and outside the body got transported here as a subconsciously familiar place from my childhood. As I say, just a theory, but it does beg the questions, where is he now and why did he contact me and summon me here?

Mrs Claus shuffled forward and brushed off flour and various crumbs from her apron, the smell of whatever she was baking was now driving everyone into a frenzy."I have a thought, "she said, "I'm thinking that we may find more answers back over at the Rainbow quarters, after all, Merlin, it was created to your specification, whatever part of you was here supervising that build, perhaps clues have been left there and you'll figure more out by looking around? You also had an office of sorts there which may be an ideal place to start?"

"Brilliant, "Merlin agreed, "I think you're absolutely bang on the money, let's do that if we're all in agreement?" The boys all agreed while still trying to get through their auto-refilling hot chocolates.There was no disagreement from the four ladies, so everyone got their winter clothing back on and braced for the cold.

"Oh you don't want to go on foot again", Santa chuckled. "I suggest you take the closet which the other Merlin installed just through here as a charming little nod to his old friend, 'Jack'".

"Jack as in 'C.S.Lewis' Jack?" Merlin asked.

"Yes, well, given that not only did the other you realise where we are based here and of course a very young Jack was also a resident here all those years ago, it seemed a fitting tribute".

"Aha, so that's where he got the ideas from, always write about what you know is what is said, so whilst fantasy has to come from the imagination, sometimes it's better to use something like a known location as a base for things. Yes, I agree with myself, a closet of sorts sounds very fitting, I suppose a wardrobe would be a little obvious, though I did set up a closet/wardrobe situation back at Gwen's house, much to the amusement of Kelly's husband Ian, and indeed the boys, so it looks like both parts of me were thinking along the same lines. Tell me where does the closet lead to?"

"Another closet installed in your office over at the Rainbow quarter, with your prior permission, of course, we use it frequently".

"Splendid, lead on, Sir"

"Young Tim, you're in charge of showing everyone around again, that's if you don't mind of course?"

"No I don't mind, of course, Santa" came the reply. Merlin, the four ladies, the three boys and of course Mrs Claus followed Santa and Tiny Tim through a wide closet door instantly into what could have been a hidden room. At the opposite wall was another wide door which Santa went forward to and opened fully. The closet was then filled with colour.

"Okay everyone, keep together, you are now entering Merlin's office, please touch nothing. It has been preserved exactly as it was when he last used it, just in case he came back which of course he now has, now, we need to go through the far door of this office and we will enter the main courtyard of the Rainbow quarter, don't forget if you get lost or have any questions, you have me, Merlin, Santa and Mrs Claus for help, and everything and I mean everything is labelled here".

Merlin stopped at what was quite obviously his desk. "Oh!" he exclaimed, "my pencil sharpener, I've been looking for this everywhere, very useful and brilliant invention." He picked up a device which had two finger operated sprung clamps, one end which held the pencil in place and a handle which you turned the opposite end. Quite different and more mechanical than modern sharpeners. "I wonder how it ended up here, must be something to do with the other me, because I certainly didn't bring it here, at least I don;t think I did. Oh dear, very troubling".

"Are you ok, Merlin?" James asked.

"Yes thank you, lad, just slowly losing what marbles I have left".

"I'll help you find them if you like?"

Merlin put his arm around James and gave him a quick hug, "Thank you, most appreciated, we should probably keep up with the others".

Tim approached Merlin, "Merlin, just a heads up, it may be worth registering the new people, I'll show you how, it's just in case you guys are all staying longer than a day or so, then at least you'll all have your own pod to sleep in".

"Good idea, tell you what, if you go and sort that while I sort something else, I'll join you presumably in my office, in just a minute or so".

"Okay Merlin, no problem, see you soon".

Merlin then approached his old friend Nicholas, "Nicholas, old chap, with reference to spirits, are spirits able to exist interactively here then? Only you mention your Father and Grandfather and potentially me and the children".

"Oh yes, Think of this place as a sort of limbo between heaven and earth, a sort of holding place for children, hence why the other you agreed we should make it as magical and wonderful for them as possible".

"I agree with the notion entirely, I only ask, because a thought occurs to me". At that moment there was a loud but familiar sound to Merlin coming from above them. "What in heaven's name is that? It sounds like, but is unlikely to be…"

"Mrs Claus stepped forward, "it's the portal being activated, a child or children are returning from somewhere, no doubt there will be the noise of welcome and stories of adventure soon".

"The portal?"

"On the roof"

"Aha, yes, the looking glass, I thought I recognised the sound, so it works then? Did I ever show you the one I have at home? Given to me by Lewis Carroll himself!In exchange for Doodle my lovely dodo, remember him?"

"Remember him? I can still hear his deafening squawk in my mind sometimes, quite sweet though, if a little loud".

Voices could then be heard of several children coming down a large flume/slide all the way to the courtyard from the roof. First to pop out was a young man who had more dirt visible than either skin or hair about him, "Merlin!" he exclaimed, "Welcome back, "he said as he stepped forward and shook the old man's hand enthusiastically, but after a second's consideration, "Are you Merlin? It's as though you don't recognise me".

"I'm afraid I don't, "Merlin responded, "I am indeed who you think I am but not as you remember me, might take some explaining".

Not to worry, "I'm Peter, also known as Peter Pan and the pile of miscreants in a pile behind me are none other than the lost boys, "Peter turned to face them, "Gentlemen!" he announced, "behind me you will notice a familiar face, but as yet he doesn't recognise us, for reasons he is yet to explain, so, stand alphabetically, and announce yourselves". The boys did exactly as asked, and said in turn,

"I'm Curly!I am 2nd in command named James! I'm Nibs! I'm Slightly! I'mTootles! And finally we are known as the twins! But occasionally we answer to Tweedledee and Tweedledum just to tell us apart you understand". All eight bowed courteously. Noah nudged Todd and James and they also stepped forward, introduced themselves and bowed in the same way.

Merlin said, "me, you know, this is my daughter Bertha, my Grandmother Katy (long story) two of my descendants Gwen and Zoe and cousin to Gwen's husband and not forgetting Mother to James, Kelly". The four women stepped forward and performed a sort of awkward curtsy/bow. "And furthermore, Santa you already know of course, but we have recently learned that Mrs Claus is in fact my Sister Ganieda which would explain how she and Zoe resemble each other so closely, this is not just coincidence, they are in fact related!".

"Amazing," Peter said, "so much to tell you, Santa. Noah, Todd and James was it? Are you all staying here? Where are you all from? Do you know?"

Noah stepped forward, Todd and I are brothers and we are from Swindon in Wiltshire, England. Our cousin James is from just outside London in the county of Surrey".

"Hi, "said Todd, "sorry to interrupt but if you are Peter Pan, where's Tinkerbell?"

"Oh grief, boys, we left Tink behind in our rush to escape Sherwood, did anyone see her come through the portal?"

"I'm coming, I'm coming, be patient!" came a girl's voice along with the sound of someone hitting and bumping every bump of the slide on her way down the same way the others had arrived and then, sure enough, a girl with glowing wings covered in leaves and twigs in her golden hair landed with a bump in front of everyone.

"Tink! You made it, wow that was all a bit close wasn't it!" Peter said giving her his hand to help stand up. The lost boys all crowded around and lifted her above their heads like a hero who had returned from battle. Quicker introductions were made than before. Merlin then said to Bertha, "could I ask that you send a message to your William and ask him if he can ask in particular Dickens, Lewis and

Barrie to join us here, if such a thing is possible, if there is doubt I'm sure we can think up a solution between us".

Bertha sent the following.

Hello my love, as you will hopefully see on the tracker thing we have safely arrived and Dad sends a message, if possible, could in particular, Charles Dickens, Jack, Lewis Carroll and J.M Barrie consider joining us here, there's too much to tell you by a text message, Dad also says if they're unsure how they would make the journey, he's sure you and he would think of something between you. Miss you, love Bertie xx

----

Hi, yep I can sort that, your signal is weaker than expected, but for some reason, your Dad's is a lot stronger, leave it with me. Miss you too, love William xx

----

"Dad, Zoe, "Bertha began, "I've heard from William, all is okay, he says he'll sort out what you asked, Dad and said something about for some reason your signal is far stronger than mine but he can't figure out how or why".

"Ha ha!" Merlin laughed, "still got a good bit of magic and pizazz in me, brilliant it worked!"

"What did?"

"Well back at the games room when I disappeared for a bit I went up to the observatory, I applied a dose of magic and good old-fashioned know-how to William's technology, boosted the power and the signal, I fear I may have to demonstrate and teach him a few bits because the combination of his technical skill and my magic and

133

knowledge could be mind blowing. Can't wait!" he said with his eyes twinkling again, "right, what's next?"

"If I may?" came the voice of Tiny Tim.

"Certainly, "Merlin replied, "apologies I was supposed to join you in my office wasn't I, got caught up with more excitement, did you know Peter Pan and the lost boys are here?"

"Yes, I saw them coming back on the portal tracker, I assume everyone has returned safely and in the good condition they left in?"

Peter and his lost boys all responded positively.

"Tim, "said Peter, "you must join us next time. It was so exciting, it was all there just like in the books and legend. Tink here only just made it out in one piece, such good luck she can fly!"

"Oh Peter, "Tinkerbell spoke up, "you do embellish such drama in your storytelling, I was fine, it's just the Sheriff's men were getting a bit angry when the boys started piling in to the castle, but the good news is we found Maid Marion and I managed to provide enough distraction to help a speedy getaway in to the forest".

Noah had a question but was unsure how to ask it, so instead it came out as a pile of unconnected words and names, "Sheriff? Forest? Nottingham? Maid Marion? Getaway? Robin Hood?"

"I can explain this one, "Tim responded, "So I actually helped orchestrate this particular adventure. Basically, Peter and the lost boys, having defeated Captain Hook and his men, the crocodile etcetera, they were feeling a bit glum and needed a new adventure, so I suggested they go to the library which I highly recommend by the way, it works differently to regular libraries, in that it can suggest things based on your mood as well as your preferences and has a host of interesting people that will read for you if you can't or don't wish to, you can also extend these facilities to your pod, I do love a story at bedtime, anyway, Peter came back to me to say they had discovered a book all about Robin Hood and his Merry Men who lived in Sherwood Forest as outlaws, this appealed greatly to them, so would I help them create that as an environment they could participate in. So, we used the games room to create it, the AI assistant is still, in my opinion, one of Merlin's greatest creations that I have ever seen. Anyway, back to what I was saying, I sent Peter and the boys off to Sherwood, Peter of course was Robin Hood, the lost boys became the Merry Men, Tinkerbell became like a sidekick but was able to use certain magic, Experience was to include the Sheriff of Nottingham, Maid Marion, Guy of Gisborne and a village full of poor people and the Sheriff's men. The Games room is plugged in to the portal so it was better to use that, we find it more stable that way. While I think of it. I'm not sure how long you're looking to stay here but shall I show you how to find your accommodation? Us children have pods on the upper floors which you can reach by stairs, elevators, climbing or whatever else you might come up with. Any adults are all down here on the ground floor. So Noah, Todd and James, let's pop upstairs. The idea is that you simply walk up to a pod door and the AI treats the pod like a virtual bedroom of sorts though it's more like having your own tenement apartment. As you approach the door it will recognise you. I've already registered you all. It will confirm your name and the doors will open. The pod will already be highlighted to reflect your favourite colour. So if I go first, you are all welcome to come in and have a look".

Tim walked up to the first pod which activated itself and a soft voice spoke "Welcome, Tim, is this the name you wish to be known by?"

"Yes, that's fine, thank you" Tim answered.

"Do I spot that you have guests with you?"

"Yes I do, they are welcome in my pod".

"Very good, could all guests step forward to the door one at a time for identification please", Noah went first being the eldest, "Hello Noah, welcome to the Rainbow Quarter I believe this is your first visit, is Noah the name you are happy to use? You can always change it later".

"Erm, yes that's fine, thanks" Noah replied.

"Very good, welcome to Tim's pod, next guest please step forward". Todd went next then James, both confirmed their names and then the door to Tim's pod slid open sideways to reveal a hallway. Everything was highlighted in green, which was Tim's favourite colour. There were four doors to choose from. Living room, Kitchen and Bathroom. Tim ushered everyone into the living room. "We may as well start in here, "he said, "I'll give you a tour in a minute. All rooms are accessible from all rooms if that makes sense, so for instance, if you want anything from the kitchen that's this door here. All rooms and doors are labelled. You can also ask the windows to show different views, so I have London how I remember it from the main window on this side, "he said pointing, " and the other window shows the courtyard downstairs where we just were". There were other children there now, but the adults had gone back into Merlin's office briefly before going on to show Bertha, Katy, Zoe and Kelly their pods. The boys in Tim's pod did a running tour, getting more and more confused. The ability to step from one room to another without going into the hallway first really messed with their internal compasses, but it was very convenient once you got used to it. To their surprise there was a sudden doorbell ring, they made their way to the front door. On the wall was a screen which showed an image of the corridor outside and indeed the person who was ringing the bell.

"Oh!" Todd exclaimed, "It's Lucy!"

"Ok, answer the door please, "Tim commanded.

There were two chimes from somewhere which signalled that there was now two-way communication from inside and outside Tim's front door "Hello, Lucy, how can I help you?

"Hi, Tim, it's Lucy"

"I know that, I can see you"

"Aren't you going to let me in?"

Tim took a deep breath and said "Computer, please open the front door, I give my sister permission to enter".

The door slid open to reveal Lucy with a big grin on her face. She spotted Todd immediately, "Toddy!" she threw her arms around him and he hugged back, "Hi Lucy, we wondered where you were".

"Hi Tim, Hi Noah, Hi James, lovely to see you all, "she hugged each one of them in turn, "so, what have I missed?"

"Well, "Todd began, "So we're here with Merlin, though technically he's not the same Merlin you've met, well he is and he isn't, it's complicated but here's a thing, Merlin, is Mrs Claus' brother! I know! Oh and we came here through the games room again where we all met.This place is amazing by the way. We've already met Peter Pan and the lost boys!"

"You've got a lot more to meet, but anyway, first things first, welcome to the Rainbow quarter. By now I assume you've got a good idea of how pods work, so, on the screen by the front door you can bring up contacts like all your friends here and you can then ring their doorbell via it, when the other person responds, it will open both your doors and provided you're given permission you can simply enter their pod. Just like I have here, it may have looked like I was standing in the corridor but no I was stood in my own pod's hallway. It's a far better facility than we had before, we never dreamed of such luxury. Our whole family lived in a single room back in London, oh how our luck has changed, Tim, so why are you all here now?"

"Again with complicated" Todd answered.

"Oh ok, I'm sure it'll all make sense soon, is it just the three of you visiting with Merlin?"

"Er no, our Mum, her sort of cousin ,Zoe, James' Mum, Kelly who is Dad's cousin, Merlin's daughter Bertha and Merlin's Grandmother, Katy are here too, we left them all downstairs".

"Oh okay, maybe they're being introduced to their pods too, I imagine that's what's happening anyway".

Lucy was absolutely right, Merlin's pod was part of his office space which he had made sure was added so it was a larger pod than the rest as it included the office as well as the normal layout, he was busy familiarising himself with it all while the ladies were shown how pods work by Mrs Claus. They approached the first pod available, Gwen volunteered to go first and as instructed she stepped forward, the voice said "Hello I'm afraid I don't recognise you, please state your name and I can try and help you"

"Hello, my name is Gwen"

"You are Mother to Noah and Todd?"

"Yes that's correct, how did you…"

"I am programmed to read your DNA as part of the identification process"

"I think I can guess what's happened, "Mrs Claus exclaimed, "I imagine young Tim registered the three boys but didn't think to add the adults, I'd be interested to know how Merlin is getting on given his DNA is the same but he's not the Merlin who had this place built so I wonder if the other Merlin put in a failsafe, anyhow, let's get you sorted and register everyone, Computer, could you take us through to reception please?"

"Certainly Mrs Claus, if everyone could step through the door you tried to enter before and state your names in turn for identification purposes, please". Each woman did so, when Bertha announced herself, the computer voice announced "Bertha, daughter of Merlin, you are most welcome indeed to the Rainbow Quarter"

"Well, that answers that then, "said Mrs Claus, "Merlin must have been registered ok or recognised".

"Correct, "the computer voice answered, "Merlin can be found in his office space at this moment, would you like to visit him?"

"No, no, we need to get these ladies registered at reception, pronto!"

They walked through into what looked like the lobby of a high class five star hotel but still in-keeping with the rainbow coloured theme of the quarters as a whole. A very attractive blonde young woman in her early twenties was stood behind what could be assumed as the welcome / reception desk.She looked up from a large book resting in front of her,

"Good day to you all ladies, my name is Summer, how may I assist you today?"

"Gosh," Gwen took a quick breath, "Gosh, humour a mad woman, you look so familiar, I just can't figure out why, I believe we need to register with you in order to stay here?"

"I'll sort this, Gwen, " Mrs Claus stepped forward to the desk. Hello, Summer, dear, I trust you are well?"

"Yes thank you, and you?"

"Oh yes, it's that time of year again, things are starting to get busier, and to top things off nicely, we have guests, now, Merlin you will know about already and hopefully three boys named Noah, Todd and James are already registered courtesy of Tiny Tim?"

"Yes indeed, I can see them all on the system they're currently in Tiny Tim's pod along with his sister Lucy".

"Oh how lovely, new friends, always wonderful. So, to add to your list if you would please, are these four women, they each require an adult pod on the ground floor, full access to everything if you would, their names are Gwen, who you've just spoken with, Katy, Zoe and Kelly. I shan't bore you with the details of how they are all connected to one another, but if it interests you I'm sure the computer will figure all that out from their DNA and you'll be able to look at it for yourself".

"I may well do that, okay, you're all good to go, just find a vacant pod, walk up to it, the computer will guide you through the rest" Summer tapped a few more keys on her computer keyboard and closed the large book in front of her".

"Sorry to bother you, my lovely, don't want to interrupt if you're busy?" said Gwen.

"Not at all, how can I help?" Summer replied.

"Bless you, a daft question really but I'm still getting used to all the things here and how it all works, but would it be rude if I asked if you're real or are you AI like the computer I was speaking to before?"

"No I'm perfectly real, I have lived here literally my whole life, I arrived here as a small baby and volunteered to work wherever needed, I love it here".

"One last question, can I give you a hug?"

"Yes of course". Summer made her way round to the front of the reception desk and opened her arms. She and Gwen hugged tightly. When the hug broke between them, Gwen had tears in her eyes but was smiling.

"Are you okay, Gwen?" Summer put her arm around Gwen again to comfort her.

"I'm okay honestly, I'm not sad, these are happy tears, I suppose I'm just a little overwhelmed by the events of the last few days, Thank you for being so kind. I'm just being silly more than anything. I guess I'm missing my husband, but not too much you understand. Everyone has been so wonderful, you, Merlin, Santa and Mrs Claus, anyway, I'll stop holding you up, you need to get on, gonna go check out my pod, not a sentence I ever imagined saying, but it's all exciting isn't it" Gwen sniffed loudly, shook herself as if to mentally shake off any lingering emotion and made for the door, "come on girls, let's go find our pods"she said passing the other three that were waiting"

"Bye everyone", Summer called out, "don't forget I'm just here if you need anything or you can call me from your pod" she waved feeling a slight rush of emotion herself, it was quite the little moment but it made her smile too.

Chapter Eighteen

"The three women stepped back outside into the courtyard. The door to reception closed behind them, but when they turned back around, it was the door to a pod again, Mrs Claus beckoned Gwen forward again just as she had done before. Gwen did exactly that, the computer voice was back again, "Hello, Gwen, are you happy to continue using the name Gwen? You can change it later if you wish".

"That's absolutely fine, I registered with that name, don't want to confuse things or do anything complicated"Gwen replied.

"Very good, I assume the four of you will be occupying your own pods? I can show you the easy ways in which you can all visit each other once you're installed".

"That's fine, " Mrs Claus intervened, "with permission I'll pop in to Gwen's pod with her and get her settled, I'll do it with all of you, of course".

"Lovely, "Gwen said, "okay computer, what's next?"

"I have to have your spoken permission to allow Mrs Claus to enter"

"Oh yes of course, she's more than welcome".

"Very good. Gwen may I be the first to welcome you to not just the Rainbow quarter but your own personal pod. I shall continue speaking while you look around and discover your new living quarters, you can ask me anything at any time including asking me to stop talking"

"Thank you computer". Gwen and Mrs Claus walked through the door which closed behind them. The computer continued to talk, "Welcome to your own personal space, Gwen. Any or all aspects of the layout, design, decor, literally anything can be changed by a simple spoken command, for instance, what may I ask is your favourite colour?"

"Ooh, let's think, I'm definitely a blue girl". Instantly everything was given a blue colour. "Can I be cheeky and make some elements a little more teal in colour?"

"Certainly. You will notice several doors all of which are labelled. All rooms are accessible back here in the hallway or via another door in whichever room you happen to be standing".

Gwen stepped into the living room to find it perfectly laid out, the kitchen was joined by way of a breakfast bar and the furniture had teal and lighter blue highlights. The windows had a message written on them saying 'You can change the view from these windows to anything you wish Just ask'. "Oh you see that's clever, let's try it, Computer? Can you give me a view of romantic Paris please?" Moments later the Eiffel tower could be seen from one window and the Arc de Triomphe from the other, they were like web cams watching a live feed of life in the two locations complete with ambient sound, perfect.

"Right, you get the idea, Gwen I'm going to pop back out and help the others"

"No worries I'm going to make a coffee and just relax a bit, poke around the place, be nosey" Gwen replied.

"Good idea, darling, see you soon". Mrs Claus exited the front door to find the other three ladies chatting. "So, how are we doing out here? Gwen is getting on a treat, who's next?"

"Well, said Bertha, I'm absolutely fine, if this place was designed by my Dad I reckon I'll be fine to figure it out for myself, so either Kelly or Zoe, or I can go in with one of them, killing a lot of birds with the absolute minimum of stones, to paraphrase a well known saying".

Being out of her depth with all the magic and AI and Christmassy goings-on, Kelly decided she needed Bertha for this experience as she seemed more real, so they went up to a pod and repeated the same procedure that Gwen had done making Bertha a guest. When it came to choosing a view, Kelly requested the great wall of China. She joined Bertha in her new pod which they were able to access directly from Kelly's front door saving leaving and going in search of another pod. Bertha was already getting used to how things worked so wasted no time in redecorating her pod to look like a medieval castle with a big open fire in the living room, She used to sneak into the castle above her home in Tintagel when she was a little girl so always imagined living there. The windows showed the open sea complete with ambient sound and passing ships. Meanwhile, Zoe was getting to grips with her own pod environment, all she could think of at the time was a tropical beach at sunset, palm trees, gentle lapping water distant music, Idyllic as far as she was concerned, She yearned for a holiday somewhere so was making the most of it. There was a doorbell sound coming from Zoe's front door. She rushed into the hallway to see an image of Gwen on a little screen. "How do I?"

"Do you wish to open the door, Zoe?" asked the computer.

"Yes please, only there's no handle," Zoe replied. The door slid open letting in rainbow coloured light and Gwen was stood there.

"Zo, this pod malarkey is amazing isn't it?" Gwen remarked.

"Are you coming in or not?" Zoe asked. She gave permission for Gwen to enter once she understood that's what she had to do, after which the two women went through to the living room. Zoe was about to suggest a refreshing drink to enjoy with the tropical view when the AI voice was heard, "attention, if you are hearing this, your presence is requested in reception", simply ask for reception at your front door for instant access".

Gwen, Zoe, Bertha, Kelly, Noah, Todd and James, Tim and Lucy all heard the announcement so did as instructed and made their way to reception by the nearest front door. They all found themselves in the reception area where Merlin was waiting at the front desk talking with Summer."Aha!" he announced."Are they all here?"

"Yes!" said Summer, "I can confirm everyone you requested on the list have arrived".

"Perfect, could you just let the others know I'll be in to fetch them shortly?"

"No problem".Summer disappeared from the front desk through a door to one side. At this point Merlin did an impressive leap onto the reception desk and made an announcement to the gathered crowd.

"Hello everyone. Sorry to pull you all away from your pods but I think you'll understand why. In short we have some visitors, some requested, some unexpected. Summer, if you can hear me through there, everyone can come in now".

Summer shouted back, "Ok, sending through now". The door Summer had used before opened. Summer walked out , turned and gestured for the hidden guests to make their way out in to the main holding area where everyone who had been previously summoned by Merlin were now gathered. The first to walk out were Chris, Dave, Ian Sam and Will, Much to the delight of all, the women all found their partners, the children followed to greet their Dads.

"What are you doing here, William?" Bertha asked, "Not that it isn't lovely to see you, but, how? Why? I have many questions".

"Ok, well, the short version is, I needed to get the ghosts here like Merlin requested, so the way that was dreamt up meant I came with, so I also invited Dad and Dave and Ian of course, they were all up for it".

"So where are the spirits? Actually, don't worry, I've just answered my own question"

Everyone quickly became aware that Charles Dickens, C.S.Lewis, J.M.Barrie and Lewis Carroll were now stood behind Merlin, in front of the reception desk. Merlin, upon seeing his daughter's face, turned slowly to see the four men stood before him. Jack stepped forward and held out his hand to be shaken. Merlin smiled then looked up at his friend and said "If only, old friend, if only".

"Try," Jack replied, "things are different in this place" Jack responded. Merlin grabbed Jack's hand with both of his and shook it with enthusiasm. Everyone was amazed.

"How is this possible? I can see you, hear you and shake your hand as if you were physically here" Merlin said, shaking the hands of each spirit in turn.

"I told you before Merlin," came Santa's voice from the entrance door, "this place is a limbo between Heaven and Earth, spirits are free to interact with the living and vice versa".

"Extraordinary, Mr Dodgson! "Merlin turned his attention to the author standing on the end, he had a young lady stood with him, dressed in Victorian clothing, her brown hair raised in a bun on her head, "and who is this charming young lady?"

"Hello Merlin, this, believe it or not, is little Alice!"

"Hello, lovely to meet you, all of you" said Alice.

"Enchanting, you can't be little Alice Lidell, the one from the books about Wonderland? You'd be much older by now, though, perhaps I'm not thinking correctly in terms of time, I remember you as a little girl" Merlin remarked.

"Yes I remember you too, Charles gifted you my looking glass I seem to remember?"

"Yes indeed, I still have it, kept safe and sound in the cave network underneath the castle in Tintagel, what is more there is another atop this very building and I am told there are more all of which are used as portals by the children here. But Charles,..."

"Yes?" came the answer. "Ok, allow me to explain, so Alice was born in 1852. She was about ten years old when you met her, She lived until 1934 aged 82 but felt her 21st year was her happiest and has since chosen to remain that age in her afterlife, you can do that it seems. When I was told we had been summoned here and learned what this place was I felt it was only right to contact Alice and try and bring her along, she always had an adventurous spirit and a keen curiosity for the extraordinary, oh and the looking glass, to my knowledge there are precisely 44 of them scattered across the globe in different places, at least that's the number that keeps coming up".

"Interesting. Well, I have some very interesting people for you all to meet. Mr Dickens. I have here two children I believe will mean a lot to you. This is Tim and Lucy Cratchit. Children, this man wrote the book that you were both brought to life in so in many ways he is like a Father to you, indeed he created your Father Bob, your Mother Emily and your siblings, perhaps he should be considered like a Grandfather or old Uncle type relation?"

Tim and Lucy stepped forward and both ran at Dickens for a hug

"This is extraordinary Merlin, "said Dickens, "I think this place is wonderful, perfect for children, just as I always dreamed of for them, and the Christmas detailing is exquisite"

"I'm glad you think so, "Merlin said, "a lot was from your own descriptive writing, there is so much more for you to see". J.M.Barrie was introduced to Peter Pan and the lost boys but it quickly became apparent that there was no-one to greet Jack other than those present who knew him. "Jack, I'm afraid, given the Pevensey children didn't die in the books, they're not here, but something even more amazing lays in store for you, I'll let Noah explain"

Noah stepped forward, "Hello Jack, great to meet you properly, so, I need to show you something, Summer, is there a way of displaying a view here like we do in our pods?"

"Yes of course, see that window at the front of the reception, you can talk at it like you do in the pod" Summer responded.

"Thanks, Jack, follow me over to the window"Noah instructed, "ok, computer?"

"Hello Noah, welcome to reception, how can I help?"

"Could you change the view at this window to show the view from the top of the Rainbow quarter facing the direction of Santa's cabin"

"Certainly". The view changed as requested.

"So, Jack, do you recognise where you are? Let me give you a few clues. Over the back there you can just see smoke coming up from a log cabin, that's where Santa and Mrs Claus live and inbetween is the shuddering wood. Jack, outside is Narnia".

"Yes thank you, Noah, I know exactly where we are".

"You do?"

"Yes of course, I spent some of my childhood here, I never expected to return I must admit, but I'm so glad it's all still here. I recognised it as soon as we arrived,the Rainbow Quarter wasn't here of course, things have changed a lot, I do wonder though, now I have something to show you, and I suggest you bring your brother and cousin too".

"Oh, okay, I'd best just let Mum and Dad know, be right back". Noah ran over to his parents and declared "Hi, just letting you know I'm grabbing Todd and James, Jack has something to show us, he knew we were in Narnia all along!"

"Okay, be careful please look after the other two"

"Yep, will do, Todd, James" he called beckoning them over, "Jack wants to show us something so let's follow him and find out what it is, James don't worry my Mum is just talking to your Mum so I reckon she already knows we're off on a mystery adventure, let's go!"

"Hello boys, I've cleared my idea with Merlin, Summer and Mrs Claus who will all be joining us too in case there are questions I can't answer. Now, through the back we go, there should be a covered walkway or similar". There was! They all walked up the covered walkway until they reached a large barn. There were stacks of hay bales lining the four walls inside and in the middle were nine reindeer, just standing around. "Now, who knows all the names of the reindeer?"

All three boys threw their hands up as high as they could. "I think James should tell us, take it away young fella".

James stepped forward and recited all nine names, each corresponding reindeer stepped forward when their name was called,

"Dasher, Dancer, Prancer, Vixen, Comet, Cupid, Donner, Blitzen and of course, Rudolph". James received a round of applause from everyone, followed by Todd interrupting with, "Didn't Mrs Claus say there was a tenth much older reindeer?"

"Well remembered, young man, "said Mrs Claus, "follow me, all of you, just through here, now can you remember her name?"

"Agnes!" Todd announced. At the sound of her name a pair of antlers rose up into sight. As did a horn shape. "Una!" Todd had also remembered. The reindeer and unicorn besties got to their feet to meet the new people, especially Todd as he had called them by name".The other reindeer could be heard chatting away behind everyone like a meeting of old women, things such as, "well they seem friendly", "perhaps we should pretend not to talk", "nonsense, if they don't know by now that all animals can talk then quite honestly, here and now is the perfect time to find out". "True". "I'm going to play it safe by going up to Mrs Claus first I think, " said Vixen. "Hello, "she said in a quiet voice in case anyone hostile or silly who thought they'd heard her talk could just dismiss as something like hunger or tiredness.

"Oh, hello darling Vixen, how are you and all the others?" Mrs Claus asked.

"Oh fine, enjoying the slightly cooler weather, looking forward to 'you know what' in a couple of weeks. Comes round quickly doesn't it!" Vixen stepped forward towards Agnes and popped her head over the little barn door to Agnes' enclosure. "Hello dear!" she shouted.

"I admit the eyesight is a little foggy, young lady, but I'm not deaf, in fact if you wouldn't mind turning it down a little I would be most grateful" Agnes responded, Una huffed in agreement. Noah, Todd and James all felt a cold wet nose nuzzle into their hands as three reindeer had been brave and come forward to say hello. Noah and Todd instinctively reached for their reindeer's left ear to rub it affectionately. James meanwhile was too busy admiring the multicoloured lights draped around Una and helping Summer get more hay for their little enclosure. Merlin was considering going back indoors but couldn't help but admire the animals too. Dancer had managed to get up on a hay bale much like a mountain goat climbing fearlessly up a cliff face and announced "who's up for a quick festive sing-song?"

"Here we go again, " Comet started, "all year round, nothing to do with the season, Dancer is obsessed with Christmas songs and as you will soon witness, close harmony singing". With various mumbling huffing and under-the-breath moaning, all the reindeer gathered together. With a starting note from Una who was the lead singer, a rousing rendition of 'Ding dong merrily on high', with opportunity for everyone to join in if they knew it, led by Dancer who was obviously the choir leader. Rudolph even got to do a solo part. From nowhere a table had materialised covered with plates of tasty festive treats such as mince pies, chocolate, christmas cakes, pudding and a machine which dispensed hot chocolate and mugs with everyone's name on. Mrs Claus denied all knowledge of how it got there but pointed at Summer quite a lot. The boys found a hay bale to sit on and enjoy their selection from the table of goodies. Una and the reindeer sang some more Christmas songs to entertain everyone.

"Summer?" Santa approached.

"Yes, Santa?" Summer replied.

"Are we ready for later for the 'you-know-what'?"

"Oh! Yes! Everything is in place as requested, everyone knows where to be and when, though it's probably worth geeing everyone in here along a bit, time is getting away from us".

"Very good, could you make some sort of announcement to that effect?"

Chapter Nineteen

"Um, yes, ok, no problem, bear with". Summer climbed on the hay bale with Una and waited for the current song to end. "Una and the reindeer everyone, big round of applause. Now a quick announcement, this evening we have a special event over in the Rainbow Quarter ballroom which is due to start in about an hour so if everyone would care to make their way back to reception and from there, back to your pods where you will find suitable attire for the occasion. Boys, you will also find a selection of new clothes in your wardrobes. To the gentlemen with partners already here, I have already taken the liberty of adding your names to the register and you are sharing pods with your partners, your partners will show you how it all works. As always, any problems you can contact me in reception either in person or by way of your pod's AI who can also answer most questions. Spirits if you would care to report to reception for further instructions. Thanks everyone".

"Summer, quick question?"

"Hello Todd, yes?"

"Are we allowed to take some of these goodies back to our pods?"

"Yes of course, though, what might be easier is you can ask the AI in your pod for any food or drink you would like and where you'd like it, you'll get used to it eventually, it's a brilliant system Merlin's created there".

"Yes it is!, Brilliant, thanks!" A quick hug and then Todd rushed over to tell the others the good news. The three of them got going pretty quickly, running mostly all the way, they all found a pod, entered the usual way, Noah's pod was pink, a favourite colour of his in recent times, the AI had picked up on it whereas both Todd and James had chosen Blue, T, just like both their Mums who were both fond of the colour without either of them knowing. The boys made their way to their individual wardrobes. They all instinctively asked the AI to show them clothes for that evening, all were presented with several options. Meanwhile Gwen and Dave, Zoe and Chris, Bertha and Will, and Kate and Sam were exploring their new accommodation previously set up and in part designed by the women earlier that day in their ground floor pods.

"So William? What do you think?" Bertha asked.

"This place is lush, Bert" he replied.

"Erm, Bert? No no I don't think so, Bertie I like, Bertha if you must but never Bert. I decided to go with a mediaeval castle theme. Right, I need to explore my dress options, wait in the living room explore the place, it's *ours* so if you want to change anything, please do but be prepared for me to disagree with your choices, "she laughed, "only kidding, I think it would be fascinating to see how you would add your own touches, oh and be a dear and light the fireplace in there would you? I always thought of fireplaces being quite romantic, oh, a quick hint, you can ask the AI to do things like lighting the fireplace. See you in a minute", she gave him a kiss on the cheek to send him on his way then disappeared into the bedroom. Will did as asked and found the door labelled 'living room'. Plush seating was found, views of the sea from the window and sure enough there was a large fireplace in there, "Erm computer?" he tried.

"Hello Will, how can I assist you?" the A.I answered.

"Erm, Bertie asked me to get the fireplace lit, I mean, could you please light the fire?"

"Certainly, there you go. Please be careful not to get too close, the flames are quite real".

"Understood, oh computer? Where is the kitchen? Actually never mind just spotted the door with the word kitchen on it, thanks anyway". Will made his way into the kitchen to find a cold refreshing drink. He opened the fridge which was fully stocked with a wider variety of drinks than you can imagine. 'Aha' he thought, he had found lemonade, then a familiar voice called out, it was Bertha. "Will? Where are you?"

"I'm just in the kitchen", came the reply, "can I get you a drink?"

"Oh, yes please, surprise me".

"Ok". Will poured another lemonade and took both drinks back through to the living room. Bertha was stood in front of the fireplace dressed in a red ballgown.

"Wow, Bertie, that was quick!"

"Oh I can be, especially when the first dress I found was definitely the one I would want to wear,I love it".

"Honestly, Bertie, you look beautiful, the dress is perfect on you".

"Thank you, William, what drink did you get?"

"Well, I was drinking lemonade so thought I'd get the same for you, hope you like it".

"Yes, thank you,I have only tried fizzy drink a few times, that was with Katy. Right I think time is running out, go get dressed, there's a closet, wardrobe sort of thing in the bedroom, you can ask th A.I to show you options".

"Yes I remember Summer saying, won't be long". Will entered the bedroom directly from the living room and began looking through his options of attire for the evening. Tuxedo seemed to be the only choice really, but went with a glittery red waistcoat given the general theme of the place and to make an effort to match Bertha's dress in some little way. When he went back into the living room to show Bertha, she approved greatly.

"Gosh, William, very smart, I will be very proud to be on your arm this evening".They both left via the front door directly to reception where Summer was waiting to point everyone in the right direction. An almost identical scene had just played out in the other three pods. Both Gwen and Kelly were in blue ball gowns but the A.I. had been clever enough to keep the styles and colour shades different enough so as not to cause argument. Zoe was dressed in yellow which she felt went best with her black hair, Chris wasn't arguing.

Meanwhile it was noted by everyone that Summer who was dressed in a rainbow coloured ball gown looked simply stunning.

"Oh, Summer, you look amazing, my dear, doesn't she Dave? Actually don't answer that", Dave simply smiled. Each of the men had chosen the same colour as their partner's dress except Chris who had gone with a green waistcoat, he felt it was a more festive colour and as luck would have it went with the yellow of Zoe's gown very well. The boys had all gone with their size of tuxedo also, all with waistcoats which matched the theme of their pods. Though Noah felt pink might not quite work and after some deliberation chose to match the whole building's theme and went with a rainbow coloured waistcoat. They all agreed to meet in Tim's pod before going down. They were also joined by Tim's sister Lucy who was wearing a very pretty green ball gown. They all agreed it would be a good idea to make their way to reception before parents and other adults came looking for them. Upon arrival, the first one to notice Summer was Noah, mostly because they unintentionally matched in their rainbow themed outfits. The children including the three boys and Lucy were met by the adults saying things such as, "Oh look, aren't they smart!", "So sweet", "Oh look the little ball gown, so pretty, a proper little lady", "young men already". Todd spotted Gwen and said, "Wow, Mum! You look amazing!"

"Thank you, Todd, you've better manners than your Father!"Gwen commented, throwing a side glance at Dave.

"Doesn't he like it?"

"He does but I'm thinking it's for all the wrong reasons".

"Oh!" said Todd pretending to understand. He was unphased, he was just in need of a snack as usual. Everyone was ushered into the ballroom through a door just at the side of reception.

Chapter Twenty

Needless to say, the ballroom was immense, each wall lined with archways, each of which contained a mirror to enhance the size of the room. At one end was a stage upon which stood Santa himself in front of a microphone.Once everyone was in, Santa leaned toward the microphone,

"Good evening everyone, I'm glad you could all make it. I have brought you all here to make a little speech, I hope you'll indulge me. After which I am told we have music and dancing while the room is transformed with tables for everyone to sit at and enjoy a wondrous meal prepared by the finest chefs and cooks the afterlife could provide. There are diagrams on every wall showing the seating plan, just like a wedding really, to show who you are sat with, it won't matter if you chop and change this arrangement, nothing is set in stone so to speak. So let's not delay. I can already spot some hungry little eyes in the crowd. Now,firstly a little announcement, as some of you know already, Mrs Claus and I have a significant wedding anniversary approaching, which we intend to mark in several ways which include taking our long awaited honeymoon which we never got to have when we married all those years ago so we are taking an extended honeymoon which will include us taking advantage of the opportunity, to retire". There were audible gasps from the crowd, "yes, it is true that the time has come for us to hang up our red coats, our hats, our boots and dust off the sleigh to prepare for our replacement. No Todd, we are not dying, we're just incredibly old, tired and would like to hand the reins over to a suitable heir while we have control over it. This brings me to my next point. As you will also know, Mrs Claus and I have never been blessed with children of our own, and indeed further to that, no descendants, yes it is true that carrying on tradition has meant we have instead been caring for the children of the world, this world, the next and others for several centuries now, just like my Father did and his Father before him, my grandfather the original 'Old Saint Nick', so we have been in discussion about who should inherit this great tradition, someone who cares greatly for others, I'd like to call to the stage for this moment my Father who I affectionately call Santa Senior and my Grandfather 'Old Saint Nick'". The ballroom erupted into applause when the two spirits joined Santa on stage. Once the applause had receded enough for him to be heard, Santa continued, "as I was saying, we, the three of us along with Mrs Claus have been discussing an obvious candidate to carry on the mantle of the Santa title. Someone who embodies the spirit of Christmas, is caring and kind and above all trustworthy. Obviously we would be popping in occasionally just to make sure things are running smoothly and help if help is wanted or needed. The person we have chosen is in this very room and is someone that is not tied to having family to worry about given that everyone here is their family.. That's not to say there is any rule preventing this person pursuing having a family of their own one day, an heir even, to hand this all down to when they feel the time is right just as we are doing now. We hope you will all agree with our decision, it has not been easy, the right person doesn't just appear every day, though this one sort of did"

"I know who it is!" Todd shouted, all knowing as ever.

"No you don't, Todd, don't interrupt Santa!" Noah barked with embarrassment.

"I do know, Noah, it's Summer!"

The room went absolutely quiet. Suddenly applause could be heard by just a few people but that gradually grew to most of the room. Summer was nowhere to be seen, she was hiding in a little spot tucked away in one of the arches, she didn't know what to think, tears started to fill her eyes.

"Todd, "Santa began again, "please come forward to the stage", which Todd did, slowly, somewhat worried that he was probably now in trouble. Santa spoke softly but so everyone could hear him,he lifted Todd on to the stage. "Tell me young man, what made you shout out that name?"

"Sorry Santa, I didn't mean to",

"Oh you absolutely did, please don't worry, you're not in trouble at all, shall I tell you why?"

"Why?"

"Because, somehow and I really don't understand how, though I do have an inkling" he said turning to Merlin who was also on the stage comforting his sister, "Todd you were right to call out, perhaps a little impetuously, but you were absolutely right. Summer?" He called out. "Where are you my dear? Has anyone seen Summer? Usually she's directly with someone when she is called".

"I'm here, Santa" came Summer's voice from the side of the stage. Santa beckoned her to join him on stage which she did cautiously, wiping away tears to save her embarrassment.

"Ladies and Gentlemen, Boys and girls, "Santa continued holding his arm around Summer's shoulders, "this outstanding young lady came to us twenty-one years and six months ago as a brand-new baby, having been denied a real-world birth and has been with us ever since. In the real world she did not even survive long enough to know if she was a boy or a girl so we let her choose, which she did within the first year, we asked her once she was old enough to talk, why she chose to be female. Her answer was simple, she had always, for as long as she could remember of her short life that far,considered that Summer sounded far more like a girl's name than a boy's and so it helped her decide.Her whole life she has shown kindness and caring. Looking after people at reception became the perfect occupation for her, helping new arrivals, helping people who sought answers, the human touch needed when artificial intelligence just wouldn't do the job. Because of everything you are my dear, we wish to hand over everything that is Christmas, to you. We of course realise you may feel a little overwhelmed at this precise moment, and there is absolutely no pressure to take this position, but let me tell you, we believe in you one hundred percent, all the way".

A"yes, absolutely, we all agree" could be heard from the two older spirits on the stage.

Summer took in the deepest breath she could muster, wiped away more tears, took the microphone from Santa and turned to address the audience.

Chapter Twenty One

"Erm, hello everyone" Summer started nervously, "I don't need to tell you how awkward I feel right now however, I live for a challenge, I am deeply honoured that I have been asked to step up to this huge role I will admit I am somewhat overwhelmed. I promise I will do my level best not to let any of you down, from now on you may still call me Summer but my other title will be 'Miss Claus' unless of course anyone thinks up anything better. Now briefly stepping back into my previous role as Summer the receptionist, I'd like to welcome our very own in-house orchestra to give us a christmas concert to dance to, I'm told requests are permitted on the understanding that there's a chance not everyone's request will be honoured. I have taken the liberty of lining the walls with chairs to sit on and soon there will be snacks and drinks available to keep you all going. Thank you all again so much". Summer handed Santa back the microphone and threw her arms around Santa and Mrs Claus saying, "thank you, Mum and Dad. Thank you for believing in me I won't disappoint you, hopefully anyway, love you both" she giggled through happy tears.

  An orchestra had meanwhile gathered on stage and were joined by Una the Unicorn who naturally had volunteered to sing. Summer climbed down off the stage and was surrounded by children who all came over to congratulate her. Noah made his way over to help her by breaking up the crowd. He asked Summer if she would dance with him, which she gracefully accepted, they were the first two on the dance floor. Gwen with a single tear in her eye nudged Dave, "oh look, doesn't he look grown up? They look so lovely together".

  "Do behave yourself, Gwen, "Dave replied, "she's 21, he's 12 he'll get his heart broken no doubt".

"Oh don't ruin it, just take in the moment, ooh, hang on, must take a photo", Gwen then retrieved her phone she had made sure she still had with her and took the photo.

Meanwhile, Todd could be found sat on a chair near the stage tucking into a mince pie. Lucy plucked up enough courage to walk over to him. Being a proper little Victorian lady she simply held out her hand and said, "Toddy, would you care to dance?".

Todd rammed what was left of his mince pie into his mouth and just managed to swallow it all before saying, "yes please, Lucy, hang on, "he reached for his apple juice to wash down the mince pie with, "okay, done", the pair hugged and shuffled awkwardly about the dancefloor. Lucy explained that she had been shown dancing by her parents, so knew roughly how it worked. She placed Todd's hands on her waist then she put her hands on his shoulders which was all in all a much more comfortable and less messy arrangement. James who had been sat with Todd, also tucking into a mince pie had been spotted by Alice who walked over to him, "Good evening James, might I have the honour of this dance with you?"

James' response was simply to put down his mince pie, stand up and say "erm, yes please".

The pair joined the others on the dance floor. Gwen was once more climbing onto chairs and whatever she could find to get the 'perfect shot'"Look Dave, our babies, isn't that precious? Dave? Oh for crying out loud, Kelly?"

"Hi Gwen" Kelly responded.

"Look at our babies, Kel, so proud, don't worry, got some great snaps, your James is looking handsome with young Alice there, how long are you going to wait to tell him she's 21 like young Summer there? Though technically, I know time works differently here but in 'real-world' terms she's 171 years old so it's somewhat like dancing with someone's grandmother"

"It won't matter, I'm more worried about Todd, Lucy is fictional after all".

"That's fine, at least they're the same age".

"This conversation is so bizarre"

"Really is" they both started laughing.

"I wonder if any of your photos will be visible in the 'real world'?

"Ooh, good point, I do hope so, they'll just have to be preserved here, when she's not dancing with my eldest I'll ask Summer about it.
The dance floor was now full to the brim with people dancing but Summer needed to bring the dancing to a stop for a while. She whispered in Noah's ear, "thank you for rescuing me, Noah and for the lovely dance, I just need to jump on stage again, I'll be back, " she got onto the stage as she had said she was going to, waited for the current song to end like she had done before in the reindeer barn then took to the microphone again, "Hello everyone, I hope you're all enjoying yourselves, huge thanks to our wonderful orchestra and of course our leading lady Una, just to let you all know that dinner is now ready. I need to ask you all to stand up against a wall or if you prefer you can stand up against the front of this stage, we need to perform a little magic".

Much mumbling could be heard as everyone did as asked. Once the floor was absolutely cleared of people, random chairs, that sort of thing, then round tables could be seen rising out of the floor, each table was decorated for the general Christmas theme. Everyone was taking the opportunity to study the seating plan. Generally all families were at together, so Dave, Gwen, Noah and Todd had their own table, Tim and Lucy were also sat at that table so they didn't need to be separated, other tables included Peter Pan and the lost boys but also included the man who created them, Mr J.M.Barrie, likewise Charles Dickens joined the table with the Cratchit children. Lewis Carroll and Alice were invited to join Kelly, Ian and James at their table while C.S.Lewis was invited to join the table of Santa Claus, Mrs Claus, Santa's father and Grandfather and of course Summer. Summer had taken the liberty of bringing a wireless microphone to the table so she could speak to the whole room easily.

"I do hope you all found where and with whom you are sat with, obviously, feel free to move around and meet each other. To really realise the magic of this evening, I would ask Mr Charles Dickens to take the microphone and read to us a section of his book which describes the food which he so wonderfully described in his book 'A Christmas Carol' if you don't mind Mr Dickens, it would be such a thrill, I have the section I speak of printed out ready for you so you won't have to recall it from memory". Charles Dickens made his way over to the table where Summer was speaking from. She suddenly produced an A4 piece of paper with the aforementioned extract of 'A Christmas Carol' printed on it, she handed it and the microphone over. Charles Dickens took both and tested the microphone by saying, "good evening, just a little note before I begin, I spent quite a time when I was alive, reading out my works at venues up and down the country so I'll be very interested to see how a modern audience responds to this. Thank you, Summer for this opportunity, this microphone invention is quite amazing isn't it! I wish it had been invented in my day".

"Oh and Mr Dickens, "Summer interrupted.

"Charles, please, " he responded with a smile.

"Oh okay, Charles, I'm sure no-one would notice or be too concerned if you embellished it a little. It's up to you".

"Ok, let's see, " as Dickens recited his work, each detail he gave became reality within the large room, making it the perfect Christmas setting.

"The walls and ceiling were so hung with living green, that it looked a perfect grove; from every part of which bright gleaming berries glistened. The crisp leaves of holly, mistletoe, and ivy reflected back the light, as if so many little mirrors had been scattered there; and such a mighty blaze went roaring up the chimney as that dull petrification of a hearth had never known in Scrooge's time, or Marley's, or for many and many a winter season gone. Heaped up on the floor, to form a kind of throne, were turkeys, geese, game, poultry, brawn, great joints of meat, sucking-pigs, long wreaths of sausages, mince-pies, plum-puddings, barrels of oysters, red-hot chestnuts, cherry-cheeked apples, juicy oranges, luscious pears, immense twelfth-cakes, and seething bowls of punch, that made the chamber dim with their delicious steam".

The room had been completely transformed, Dickens was now stood in a room of his own creation, surrounded by people he had grown to love. More children than he had ever dared to hope that he could provide for, a dream come true, he was almost overwhelmed with emotion as the room erupted in applause but he was able to take control of himself, saying "thank you all" and handing the microphone back to Summer. He lingered at the 'Christmas' table for a while as he was keen to meet everyone properly. He raised a glass to the table saying "here's to Christmas!".Everyone at the table responded by raising their glass and replying with, "Christmas!" There was a big cheer, then an army of elves materialised pushing and pulling trolleys piled with food. Everyone was able to choose as much as they wanted of whatever they wanted. Tim ran over, grabbed the microphone from Summer, saying, "I feel this is the perfect moment to say 'God bless us everyone!' The room erupted with cheers once more, Tim handed the microphone back to Summer looking guilty but glad he'd done it.

The meal continued for hours, nobody felt tired or full, just happy and full of Christmas spirit. Charles Dickens continued to read his work aloud upon the request of everyone. The orchestra continued to play but not intrusively so, in the background, more to compliment the general mood and vibe of the evening. There was a general murmur among all the children, they had noticed that it was snowing out in the courtyard, some left to go play outside but had every intention of coming back in. It just felt the right thing to do. If asked, nobody really remembers going to bed, or returning to their pods, or how or any of the circumstances surrounding it, however it was now morning, the sun was shining,there was still snow on the ground and the roof of the Rainbow Quarter and well, just about everything really. Everyone was waking up in their own pod.

"Good morning everyone, "said the A.I, "I will shortly be letting the sunshine filter through the windows for your well-being, if you do not wish for me to do this, please let me know. Also, don't forget to check for notifications, there are quite a few following last night's celebrations. The weather today is no warmer or colder than yesterday but there is plenty of unbroken sunshine with a slight chance of further snow this evening".

Noah, Todd and James all received the same notification, "When you are ready, your parents are waiting in reception, why not get washed and dressed and join them for breakfast?"

"That message was definitely written by Mum" Thought Todd, "best get sorted".

The three boys all arrived within a few minutes of each other. Summer greeted them as always.

"Hello you three, your Mums, Dads, and a few others including Merlin and Santa are all in the breakfast room just through that door where you went into the ballroom last night."

The boys entered the breakfast room to be greeted by Santa, Mrs Claus, Gwen, Dave, Kelly, Ian, Zoe,Chris, Katy, Sam, Bertha and Will. And indeed a smaller army of elves than last night, acting as breakfast servers. "Go on in, boys, "Summer said from behind them, "you can ask for literally anything you wish and the elves will fetch it for you".

The boys agreed that they would need lots of apple juice, as recommended by Noah and Todd and of course Merlin.

"Now boys, " Mrs Claus started, "Summer? Would you care to join us?"

"I'd love to, "Summer replied, "but I can't really leave the reception, I've yet to sort a replacement for me too, but I'm around obviously if I'm needed".

"Such devotion, she knows full well that the A.I. can take over the role but she insists on manning everything herself, now where was I?Ah yes, of course. I wanted to say that it's been truly wonderful having you all here, getting to meet and know you all, however, while you are all of course are welcome to come back and visit us anytime you wish, there will always be a pod and a mug of hot chocolate with your name on it, however we are about to embark on a very busy time in our calendar, Christmas, Summer's training and induction, your schooling, adult's work etcetera etcetera, so we need to discuss about returning everyone to the real world.

"But I don't want to go back to school", said Todd. "I'm guessing there must be a school here because how else do kids who arrived here as babies learn anything, like Summer?" Todd suddenly felt a pair of arms hug him from behind and give him a squeeze, the arms belonged to Summer.

"He's quite the intuitive little cherub isn't he Nick?" Mrs Claus observed, "well… "she went to continue.

"…Well, "Dave interrupted, "come on mate, I think we will all be sorry to leave but knowing we can all come back at some point is a positive in all our books". He leaned toward Gwen, "there's something else I haven't mentioned that we need to return for too" he said in a sort of mumbled 'under-the breath' way".

"Oh no, Dave, you haven't gone and spent money on anything silly again have you?" Gwen asked.

"No, of course not", Dave replied unconvincingly. "Anyway, with Merlin's help of course I hope we can all return soon!"

"Yes, certainly, I plan to return to my wife for a short spell before I start another adventure but time in terms of me returning home or anything else is irrelevant really, of course, given I can return within any time frame I please, now if I could master space as well as time, that would make everything a lot easier, Nick was always better at that than I was, I never quite fully got the hang of it, I can give it a reasonable go, but like anything, I want to master it"

"Hmmmm, " Todd started thinking out loud again, "Merlin, you do realise that if you master time and space that technically makes you a timelord, you know like with Doctor Who? It makes sense because you've also figured out how to create a space like the door in the woods, we entered a building which was much bigger on the inside than outside, and the idea of the closet in Santa's house which opens up in to your office here in the Rainbow Quarter, your observatory back in the big building in the woods, it's all tardis technology but done in a different style. In a lot of ways I think you've already got a good idea of both time and space"

"He's right, ya know, Merlin, " Santa added, "between us we've pretty much got it covered, how else do you think I get all those presents delivered each year, in one night? Well yes, technically, but it needs a little pizzazz, or, what did the lad call it? Tardis technology? I like it! " he smiled. Merlin walked over to Todd, took both his hands in his and said "thank you, lad, that meant a lot, to be helped to realise one's potential is a truly great gift, I shall stop doubting myself and make awesome happen on a more regular basis!" at which point he ruffled up Todd's hair like you would a dog, a sign of gratitude and affection.

"Now, I've had a thought, "Santa started, "regarding returning these lovely people to their lives. About this time of the year in the final run up to the 'big day', I like to give the sleigh and the reindeer a test drive, to make sure everything is in top condition for the main event, as it were. I also allow Agnes to come along too, bless her, she's older than the others, and as such her eyesight isn't what it most likely was, she can hear fine, but if she's flying with the others she won't need to navigate and we'd only be doing a short journey so she won't get too tired, I'm rambling again aren't I, my point is that the sleigh holds up to thirty people so there would be enough room for everyone, if that would help of course? I won't be offended if you'd prefer to make your own way back?"

At this point the three boys lost their minds with excitement and begged their parents to let it happen. Everyone agreed that if Santa didn't mind dropping them all off at Dan's cave where Henrietta was hopefully still parked up and safe, plans to get everyone back to where they needed to be, could be solved.

"Okay then, "Santa began, "so, Summer? I need to leave you in charge, you know where everything is and how everything works, we're not abandoning you, we will be straight back"

"Not a problem, " Summer responded. "Thanks to Merlin's innovations, this place almost runs itself".

"Indeed"

"One last favour, if we can take everyone through to the reindeer like before?"

"Certainly"

"Are we going right now?" asked Todd.

"No time like the present" said Merlin.

"Can we have ten minutes to say goodbye to our new friends?"

"Yes, of course, it'll take me a while to get the reindeer properly prepared anyway", Santa responded.

"Tell you what boys, "Summer stepped in, "why don't you go and find your friends and come back to me here at reception when you're ready?"

The boys agreed and ran out of the breakfast room before their parents had a chance to say anything such as "be careful" or "don't take too long" or "don't do anything you shouldn't" or "make good choices", in fact by the time any of these things occurred to them, the boys were already half way up to the first floor of pods, they agreed to all gather in one pod then visit their friends one by one or invite them in to where they were. Noah invited the other two into his pod, then said, "right, I reckon we invite everyone we want to see in here or even in reception? Then we have access to stuff more easily and we have a Summer to help?"

The other two agreed it was a good idea so they all went back to reception via Noah's front door. Summer was, of course, waiting. "Hello you three, back so soon?"

"Well, "Noah took the lead on this one, "we figured that it might be easier to summon people here instead? To say goodbye to I mean, are you able to send a message to people individually to get them to join us here?"

"Yes of course, I'll need a list the people you want to see"

"Right okay, off the top of my head, obviously Tim and Lucy Cratchit, Peter Pan, the lost boys and Tinkerbell, can anyone think of anyone else we've met on this trip?"Oh, is Alice still here?"

"Alice returned to England with Mr Barrie I believe", Summer replied.

"That's okay, we're more than likely to catch up with them back in Oxford sometime".

"Oh, is that something that can happen, I wasn't aware you could interact with spirits back in the real world?"

"You can't normally, but obviously with Merlin involved, nothing is ever quite normal", Noah laughed.

"Very true, let me get those others down here so we can get you three over to the reindeer". Summer did something on her computer and a message was sent straight out. In less than five minutes Tim and Lucy were the first to appear. After hugs all round, Noah explained what was happening, "we need to go home, but, it's not forever, we've been told by Santa himself that we're allowed back at any time, so we will definitely come back, our parents said we had to go back home. We will miss you and the Rainbow quarter, won't we?"

Todd and James both nodded.

"Update for you", Summer began to say, "Peter Pan, the lost boys and Tinkerbell were last recorded as on their way to catch the Hogwarts express if that means anything?"

"Wow, that's cool, "said Noah.

"The what?" asked Tim,

"Ok so the Hogwarts express is a train that leaves from London and heads north to a school called Hogwarts, which is a school for young wizards, you can read all about it in a series of books about a young wizard called Harry Potter by the author J.K.Rowling".

"Thanks Noah, I'm gonna pop to the library later anyway so I'll grab a copy of that".

"Good idea, I've read all the books, there's 7 I believe, plus another which is called 'the cursed child' which is set a few decades in the future of the original books, it's actually the script of a play which has been produced and performed at a theatre in London".

"Tim and Lucy, " said Summer", I need to take Noah, Todd and James through to where we keep the reindeer, do you want to come with us to see them too?"

"Oh, yes please!" said Tim and Lucy simultaneously. All five children followed Summer past reception, out a door at the back, along a covered walkway and into a large barn, just like had happened before. All the reindeer including Agnes were all huddled together making short work of munching through a large hay bale and some pre-prepared reindeer food made by Mrs Claus. Everyone who had been in the breakfast room was now in this barn with the reindeer. Hot chocolate was being consumed at a good steady rate. Tim and Lucy knew all the reindeer by name so went over to hug them all in turn. However, they had never met Agnes. Agnes stepped forward to meet the two children, "Hello, I hear two new voices?"

"Children, this is Agnes, she's new but older than the rest" Mrs Claus explained.

"I may be a little blind, but my hearing is in top condition, I like to think of myself as maturer than the rest, not just older, but wiser, and what are your names?" Tim and Lucy introduced themselves and offered up hugs and an ear rub.

"Where did you two learn to do that to Agnes' ear?" Merlin asked, "it was the correct one too".

"From you, silly" Tim announced cheekily.

"Well, that would make sense, I suppose."

"Ok, I reckon we're good to go" Santa announced.

"Where are you going?" asked Lucy.

"Santa is taking us home to give the sleigh a good test and make sure the reindeer are up to the challenge of Christmas night" said Todd.

"Oh, so you're about to go right now? All of you? And you're going in Santa's sleigh? Gosh, I wish we could come too". Said Tim.

Mrs Claus put her arms around both the Cratchit children and pulled them in for a big cuddle, "now children, sadly it's just not possible, it's too dangerous for you, because there's no way for you to exist in the real world, at least not that has yet been discovered, if you flew in the sleigh back to England with the others, you may suddenly vanish, we can't let that happen, you are safest here where your new friends can visit you".

"Don't worry, Lucy, I promise we'll be back again, before you know it, "said Todd.

Lucy turned to Todd and threw her arms around him, "Thank you for being the loveliest friend, Toddy, I'll miss you, and you Noah and you James, be safe and come back soon, Mrs Claus, are we able to write to eachother?"

"Yes that should be possible, in fact we know it is, because Merlin wrote to himself from here, long story".

"Shall we, Toddy? I'll write first if you like"

"Okay, yes, I'll write back of course", Todd promised.

"The sleigh, "Santa interrupted, "is just out the back of here in it's own sort of garage if you will, I've had the elves checking it over all morning for any structural issues and they've just given it the all clear so really now it's just a case of getting everyone on board, lining and hooking up the reindeer. So if everyone could follow me through, we'll get you all comfortable, Tim and Lucy you are of course more than welcome to come through and have a look if you wish".

Chapter Twenty Two

"Everyone followed Santa, elves were ready to help everyone on board. Merlin suggested he sit up top with Santa. Agnes was at the back of the reindeer group that way if she needed to stop at any point, she could just be pulled along. Una followed Agnes out to the sleigh so they could say goodbye. All the children were already climbing all over the sleigh to look at everything.

"I suggest boys, "said Santa, "if it's ok with your parents that you all take it in turn to have a go at holding the reins while we fly". The men of the group all agreed they'd love to have a go at that too if it was okay, they would then be on hand to take care of the boys, make sure they don't do anything silly, even though they were sure Santa and Merlin would have it all under control.One last hug from the Cratchits and indeed Mrs Claus and of course Summer, who were both staying behind to make sure things were in order.

"It was so lovely to meet you all, I look forward to seeing you all again soon, " Summer said to everyone now in or on the Sleigh.

"Right, everyone hang on, take-off is not always the smoothest of operations but it stabilises quickly!" Santa shouted from above. As promised the sleigh shook as it performed a vertical take-off. Santa's voice could then be heard inside the sleigh through a sort of speaker system like being on a plane, "Good day everyone, this is Santa speaking, I'd like to take this opportunity to welcome you all aboard my Christmas sleigh, I'd like to give you more details but it would be almost irrelevant given that we will be arriving at our destination almost immediately, given the ability to skip the tedious need to actually travel through physical space, could someone elect someone to tell me where you'd like to go? There is a communications device on the left of the cabin.

"I'll sort it shall I?" Dave asked. With everyone in agreement, he leaned forward, picked up what looked like an old phone receiver and spoke into it, "Hello Santa, can you hear me okay?"

"Perfectly!" came the reply".

"Okay, great, if you could make a stop by Dan the dragon's cave near Marlborough, most of us will be getting out there, Merlin knows where it is if you get stuck".

"Very good, here we go".

Moments later, Santa spoke again, "hello again everyone, have the boys decided who'd like to come up here with me first?"

"I think James should go up first, then Todd, then I'll go up with Dad, " Noah suggested.

"That's kind of you, Noah," said Kelly, "is that good with you, Todd?"

"Yeah" Todd shrugged, he was genuinely fine to go second, though he wanted to go up with his Dad too.

"Ok, "said Noah, "we're sending James up".

"Very good, I will lower a hatch at the front, just climb on through, it's perfectly safe, "Santa instructed". James managed to climb through the hatch and up a sort of ladder which led him to Santa and Merlin sat on a very comfortable seat. James' Dad Ian instinctively followed too in case there was any problem.

"Aha, welcome both of you, climb up on here, you're quite safe, now, what I've done is taken the liberty of stopping just short of our destination so that you can see the astounding view from above Wiltshire, now James, take these reins, if you pull on your left then the reindeer will know to bank in that direction, if you pull both sides they will bring us to an absolute stop, that should do you, have a practise. Now remember we are completely invisible, you can't accidentally hit anything and you are in complete control, never fear, I'm here to help if it gets tricky, one last control you have an accelerator by your right foot, just like in a car. It 's quite a clever system that does without the need for anything cruel like a whip, what it does is it activates what the elves like to call the tickler! And that's exactly what it is and does, it tickles the reindeer signalling them to fly faster".

James pulled left and so that's the direction they went in, then he tried the other way, he pushed the tickler and they went speeding over the countryside.

"Brilliant!" Santa roared gleefully, "you're a natural James! Ian, you want to watch this one, speed demon!"

"Yes quite, be careful James" said Ian.

"Don't worry, they've all been fitted with sensors, called eyes, if there's anything about to get in the way, they simply fly over it then carry on until told otherwise.

"Understood, "said Ian in an unconvinced slightly terrified tone. After five minutes or so, Santa suggested swapping everyone around, getting Dave to bring up both Noah and Todd at the same time. Like before, Santa handed the reins this time to Todd and repeated his instructions. Todd simply put his foot down firmly on the tickler and sent the sleigh and its passengers roaring over more countryside, not knowing where to aim for in particular so straight ahead just seemed like a good idea.

"Todd, why are you going so fast?" Noah asked, "we're not in any rush particularly are we?"

"Noah, "Todd replied, "this is awesome!, seriously, you have to try it!"

"I will when we've gone back for my stomach, perhaps I should take over now?"

"No!, I know what I'm doing, Noah, don't distract me or we might crash".

"Okay you two," Dave interrupted, "a few more minutes, Todd, then we need to let your brother have a go, please".

"Fine!"

Ten minutes and an impressive list of excuses and counter-arguments later, Todd gave in, threw the reins at Noah and slumped back in his seat, Noah pulled on the reins to slow the reindeer down a bit.

"Okay Santa, which way to Marlborough from here?" Noah asked.

"I wouldn't worry too much Noah, as I said before we don't need to fly through physical space so once you've had a go I'll simply be getting us straight there almost instantaneously, however, if you were to press the button just in front of you labelled 'NAV'"

Noah did exactly that, at which point a small screen popped up in front of them showing a map, like in Henrietta. Noah leant forward and pressed the little microphone icon on the screen and when prompted, he said 'Marlborough' then the screen changed to show the direction.

"Oh cool, on it!" Noah said who very lightly pushed the tickler with his foot just to get a feel for it and very casually and safely steered the reindeer in the general direction of Marlborough".

"Lovely control, Noah, " Santa observed, "you've all been such good drivers on this trip, each in a wildly different way, it's been quite exciting".

"Without wishing to interrupt everyone's thoughts, "said Merlin, "however I've just observed on the map that we are approaching Swindon which means we're not far, don't forget the Ridgeway is just south of Swindon".

"Very good, Merlin, well observed, "said Santa" in fact, boys, if you look closely we should be going past your house soon, I believe 'that' is Eldene Drive" he pointed".

"Yes!"Noah confirmed, "look Todd there's the doctor surgery, then, just over here is Morrisons, anyway right we need to head south by the looks of it on the map, wow, there's the spotted cow pub, then there's the hospital we were both born in, you don't realise how many roundabouts there are until you see it all from up here do you?\"

"Oh I was aware" said Dave, "we're about to go over the apple tree in Chiseldon, so you're gonna have to go West now, Noah, pull to the right a bit, I know exactly where to go from here, shall I take over for a minute?"

"If you want to, Dad, I don't mind".

"You've both done really well though boys, very proud, we'll make drivers of you yet!"

Dave was thrilled to get a quick go in. "Okay Santa, we're close now, just heading up the ridgeway and we need to go roughly over there where there's that clump of trees, there should be enough room to put this lot down near the cave and our car, erm, how does one land this thing?"

"Ah, well that's an entirely different ball game, "Santa said", what I suggest happens is you give me the reins, direct me in, now, when we're where you want to be, you'll see what looks like the stop on a pipe organ, or a large manual choke on an old car it should be marked 'anti-gravity', when we've come to a complete stop you slowly pull that out to lower us to the ground. Between Dave and Santa and with excited commentary from Noah and Todd, the sleigh, all of it's passengers and the attached reindeer descended perfectly in the space next to Henrietta.

"Perfect, Dave, well done everyone concerned, "said Santa, "I call that a resounding success, let's get down and give those reindeer some well deserved love and indeed food and drink, sterling effort!"

Santa re-opened the hatch for Dave and the boys to climb back down through. He got down a different way but appeared by the door everyone else had entered by.pressed a few buttons and the door opened complete with ramp for everyone to exit easily. He caught the three boys before they ran off, "could you three do me a favour? Believe it or not this sleigh has boot space at the back, in which you will find bowls, there is also a box of Mrs Claus' special reindeer food and an ever-pouring water bottle, nothing too heavy, but it's all for the reindeer, if you could help fetch it all, get some of the adults I know can hear me talking to you to help too".

The boys ran round the back of the sleigh, Noah noticed the button labelled 'open' which he obviously pushed. They were joined by Will, Bertha, Katy and Sam who grabbed as much as they all could between them and they all made their way round to the reindeer a line of other adults was forming round to the boot to grab all that was left. Each reindeer started on the water. True to Santa's description, the water bottle that the boys were pouring from, never stopped, it was an everlasting supply. Slowly but surely, all the animals from Dan's cave emerged and came to see everyone. Dan himself poked his enormous snout into the open air, "Master?" he asked

"Is that?" Santa began to ask.

"Yes, it absolutely is, "Merlin interrupted.

"Dandelion? Your 'pet' dragon, honestly Merlin, only you would have a pet so dangerous, what in the world is he doing secreted in a Wiltshire hillside?".

"That's a long story, but he's safe in there as is everyone else".

"He's not dangerous, Santa, "Todd insisted in a slightly irritated voice, "he's actually our friend and he can burp real fire!"

"Yes, I remember, "Santa responded, checking that his eyebrows were still attached, "sorry, young man, I didn't mean any offence, so Merlin, is he coming out?"

"Well, "Merlin replied, "he might do, but nobody can really make a dragon do anything, I can ask him, see if we can encourage him?"

"I'll help, " said Bertha, "I think he likes me so he might do it for me?"

"Lovely, okay, let's go say hello". They left everyone outside and walked towards the cave. They were met by Barry the badger. "Hello, Merlin,, go easy on Dan, only he's been suffering a little with a mouth ulcer so he's been grumpy for days".

"Oh, we'll sort that for him, thank you for telling me, has everyone else been okay?

"Oh yes, though the owls went quiet for a while, they're still coloured like feathery rainbows".

"Ah yes, well, that's what you get for being nosey I'm afraid. It's not a problem, it'll wear off soon, I think anyway". Right, let's go find a grumpy dragon. Merlin and Bertha could be seen holding hands as they cautiously entered the cave. A low rumble could be heard, but this was different, it was accompanied by a sort of gurgling noise, "Sorry, excuse me, "Dan said. Merlin quickly pulled Bertha to one side so they could let Dan get out of the cave. Once he was outside, Dan stood up on his rear legs, stretched, pointing his head upwards, He opened his mouth as wide as it would go and he let out a burp which could be heard for miles and which sent a huge fireball in to the sky that anyone who noticed it from nearby villages assumed it was yet another firework display for no good reason, sending all dogs barmy."Sorry everyone, needed that, if you'll excuse me" he then crouched down and carefully slinked back into his cave. The general shocked silence from the onlooking crowd was broken when Todd looked at Santa and said, "Told ya, he's awesome isn't he!"

"He's something, certainly!" Santa answered.

Meanwhile back in the cave, "Hello Dandelion" Bertha said softly, making a fuss of his left ear. We hear you've been a bit under the weather recently?"

"Yes, I accidentally burnt my inner lip from burping because I tried to stifle it and it gave me a mouth ulcer so the best way to avoid making it worse is to step outside and open my mouth properly to let nature take it's course that way, it's been quite frustrating"

"Oh, you poor thing, hang on, I have an idea, I'll be right back", Bertha popped back out of the cave but returned a few moments later holding leaves of some sort. "This will hopefully do the trick, but I'm going to need you to open your mouth and tell me where it hurts. This is an old natural remedy which I fear has been forgotten about in modern times, these particular leaves from a specific plant will give you pain relief and help the ulcer to heal, you must remember to drink more though, lovely, your skin seems dryer than normal, that won't help the healing process".

Dan opened his mouth and Bertha found the ulcer almost straight away, she gently applied the leaves she had retrieved from outside and told Dan to just rest his mouth shut for a while to let the leaves work their magic. "There's a cure or preventative for most ailments in plant life if you know what to look for. The native American Indians knew this and thankfully now so do some of us. There you go sweetheart, you rest, we're back now so no need to worry, we'll be back to check you again soon". She rubbed his left ear until his eyes became heavy which didn't take very long at all. She and Merlin left Dan to snooze in pain free comfort. They stepped outside where everyone had gathered waiting for whatever might happen next. The boys had already got themselves installed in Henrietta because it was getting cold outside being mere weeks from Christmas itself. Luckily Mrs Claus had insisted on having a machine attached in the sleigh which dispensed her hot chocolate so that was not going to waste!

"So, I reckon, in the car should be the boys, Gwen and myself, Kelly and Ian, because their car is at our house, Merlin?, but then there's Zoe, Chris, Will, Bertha, Katy, Sam which I wouldn't have room for, I can of course come back and drop people off in stages?"

"I'll stop you there, " Santa interrupted, "you forget I have a sleigh with ten, well nine and a half willing reindeer to pull it. Agnes huffed in a disgruntled manner at the 'nine and a half' remark. "Marlborough is literally just over in that direction, I can have the Marlborough contingent home and settled before you even reach the A419".

"Done! No argument from me as long as everyone else is happy with that plan?" Everyone was luckily in agreement preventing any more discussion out in the cold. So, everyone knew where they were going, those heading to Swindon got in Henrietta, everyone else got back in the sleigh. The sleigh took what felt like merely half a minute to arrive at the house in Marlborough. Zoe said, "Santa, I can't not invite you in for a drink and a mince pie, it feels rude given you're actually here, doesn't mean we won't also leave you something out for when you next visit, obviously".

"It's very kind , Zoe, but I feel I ought to get going, now, young Katy and Sam, you don't live here do you, where have you come from originally?"

"We're over in Oxford, "Katy replied, "we're happy to grab a bus back in the morning, it's not a problem".

"Nonsense!" Santa declared. "What's a quick trip to Oxford?" Five minutes in my luxury jalopy? Hop aboard. Before the reindeer change their mind, thank you all, see you soon!"

Katy and Sam jumped back in the sleigh and climbed up front to sit with the big man himself. They joined him in waving goodbye to those entering the house. Sam shouted, "Will, see you and Bertie at the pub, busy time coming up".

"Definitely, don't worry we'll scoot over soon, "Will shouted back. "William, do try not to draw massive attention to the fact there's an enormous sleigh sat outside the house with Santa actually sitting on it, and all the reindeer", said Bertha dragging him indoors, this amused Zoe and Chris no end, they smiled at each other with the idea of a woman taking control of their son.

"Don't worry, Bertie, the locals will probably think it's just drunken people making a nuisance of themselves, if they actually saw anything they'd probably never believe it or it would give them something to talk about for quite some time" Will responded.

Over in Swindon, everyone in Henrietta arrived back safely, usual routine followed, kettle on, kids upstairs, teeth, face and hands wash, bed. Kelly and Ian decided to stay another night, a decision which was helped by the fact that of course, Merlin had not been the one responsible for bringing everyone back, therefore time had not been taken into account and so they had all arrived back a day later than expected, something to do with time passing at the usual rate there in the real world whereas time in the North pole was a bit hit and miss, especially when travelling by sleigh, time tends to get ignored a bit to make it fit what you're trying to achieve. So this needed to be fixed. Gwen rang Zoe putting her on loudspeaker so all the adults could speak together, just to say that if they hadn't noticed already due to nobody's fault, a whole day had been lost and given that things like work and school for all concerned was a bit of a potential issue, Merlin had a plan to correct the problem, but were they okay with him doing that, if so, don't freak out when you see time change across everything. Everyone was in agreement that a day gained would be an opportunity too good to miss, so Merlin was told a unanimous "yes please".

Merlin said, "ok, well, if you're all sure?", he clasped his hands together, separated them then simply clicked the thumb and forefinger on both hands and in an instant, anything with the date displayed, instantly showed the day before it was just a moment ago, but it was still late at night. Despite this, three boys suddenly appeared at the living room door.

"Hi!" said Noah with a cheesy grin on his face.

"Hi!" said Todd, also looking slightly mischievous.

"Hi!" said James looking confused but ready for naughtiness at any given moment.

"No idea why but we suddenly all woke up and started laughing" explained Noah. "So we thought we'd risk it and see if there was any chance of a hot chocolate?"

"Very good idea," said Gwen, "anyone else shall I make a big pot of it? I can't promise to make it as good as Mrs Claus did, that stuff was other-worldly, but I tried to watch what she did so I have a few ideas".

A resounding "yes please" came from everyone. Gwen disappeared into the kitchen while Merlin sparked up the fire. Moments later, Gwen shouted, "Boys? Help needed in the kitchen please".

Gwen made the sensible decision to load the boys up with mugs and a few bags of marshmallows while she carefully carried the hot chocolate through, everything was put on the table.

"Oh, yes, Dave, quick word in the kitchen if you would, boys please let an adult help with pouring the hot chocolate.

Gwen and Dave disappeared to the kitchen, "so, back in grotto-land earlier, you said the words: there was something you needed to tell me about?"

"Oh yeah, I forgot about that," Dave replied.

"What did you buy?"

Dave smiled, "lottery ticket".

"Given I can tell when you're winding me up, be very careful with where this is going".

"Okay, well, so, you know I have a bit of a, not an addiction, but the occasional flutter, I thought why not, grabbed a euromillions online,

I figured as there was still a few quid left in the lottery account I'd enter us for the Friday night draw just gone".

So did we win something? Is that what you're trying to tell me?"

"Yup!"

"Ooooh, where ya taking me with your £5? Or do we have a night in and blow it on another ticket?"

"Ha ha, well, tell you what, add seven zeroes on the end of your fiver, drop the sarcasm and we'll talk, I'm off for a hot chocolate"

"Erm, dave?"

"Yes my love?"

"7 zeroes means 50 million".

"Oh I'm so glad because I had to figure that out, millions and billions are different in America, for example so it's all very confusing, luckily this is in pounds".

"Are you serious right now?"

"Very. I rang them to make cast iron sure, they give you a financial advisor so I had them set up a new completely different bank account, the money is already in there, even though we've just gone back a day, I double checked as soon as Merlin did his abracadabra"

"How on earth did you manage to wait this long to tell me?"

"I'm not sure I just wanted to make sure I didn't broadcast it to everyone within earshot. I've also considered that we have to be careful, we can't just suddenly own huge properties and fancy cars etcetera, this needs some serious thought. Which I've started doing already, obviously, but I'll wait for you to catch up, then we can plan together".

"You don't suppose 'you know who' had anything to do with it do you?"

"I doubt it, he'd have to know I'd bought a ticket first and I didn't tell a soul, I just did it quickly on a whim as I've been known to do, obviously".

Todd walked in briefly then walked straight back out again, "Don't go in the kitchen Noah".

"Why not?" Noah asked.

"Mum and Dad are kissing, honestly, time and a place, we've got guests and everything".

"Right, said Dave, when we go back in there, say nothing until we've had a chance to discuss it, just the two of us".

"Oh agreed, yes, let's get that hot chocolate".

"Yes, let's".

The boys sat on cushions in front of the fire, the two couples cuddled up while Merlin settled down in his usual armchair and told them all a story, mostly answering questions fired at him from the boys, including such pressing things as how did he and his sister meet Santa originally, how did they end up in Tintagel, where had they been before, why did they move? Merlin didn't mind talking about it but some of it was a very long time ago that even he struggled to remember some of the fine details.Noah was always quite good at staying awake, just like his Dad, and so he was usually 'last man standing', this night was no exception, Todd and James lost the battle, hot chocolate a cosy fire, Merlin's voice, are all great for sending you to sleep. They weren't being rude at all, and Merlin didn't take it that way in the slightest. Dave picked up Todd, Ian picked up James, Noah followed, but not before giving Merlin a huge hug,

"thank you, Merlin, merry Christmas".

"Most welcome, lad. Merry Christmas to you too. See you all in the morning, no doubt".

Chapter Twenty Three

Everyone woke up the next morning feeling refreshed and ready for the day, but ever-so-slightly glum at not waking up in their own pod. Merlin could already be found sat at the computer looking at timetables, bus timetables to be exact. The boys found it quite easy to get up though safe in the knowledge there was no school, though they were still quite confused as to which day it actually was. Kelly and Ian would have no say in the matter as they were asleep on the sofa bed in the living room like before. Everyone assembled first in the kitchen to allow James to go wake his Mum and Dad up before the invasion of everyone else.

"Perhaps I should go in with a coffee for them?" Gwen suggested. James liked this idea, so he gave it his approval. Gwen made her way into the living room, and whispered as quietly as she could but not so quiet that she wouldn't be heard, but not so loud that made either or the both of them jump which would make her jump, therefore spilling coffee everywhere. She had thought about this way too much. The matter was taken care of by the front doorbell ringing and Dave shouting, "on it!" which he was, it was a parcel no doubt from Gwen's ongoing Amazon addiction and some letters. Anything in a brown envelope was carefully separated from the pack and put in a drawer in the kitchen, mentally labelled 'Deal with later'. One for me, two for Mum, one for Todd.

"For me?" asked Todd. He opened the letter to notice some glitter falling out of the envelope. Then he remembered, if anything like Merlin's letter he got from himself that time, by closing the envelope and then opening again shortly all the glitter would magically be back in the envelope meaning no cleaning up.

"So, " Gwen started, "What do people want for breakfast? Are we thinking simple like cereal or toast or would people like it cooked?"

Everyone was so keen to get on with the day, simple was the aim of the morning, so many hands making light work meant several boxes of cereal, a stack of toast, various spreads and jams, and jugs of fruit juice.

"I was looking at buses again, this morning, "Dave," Merlin said, "if I can get a lift into Swindon, when you're ready, there are regular buses so I'm happy to loiter until I find one that takes my fancy".

"Certainly Merlin, are you venturing to Oxford?"

"That's my thought, yes".

Gwen's phone started ringing, it was Zoe.

"Hello, Zo, everything alright?"

"Hi Gwen, yeah, all good, how about you?

"Yeah, just doing breakfast, I think I've just heard, Merlin is looking to grab a bus to Oxford or something".

"He might want to wait for a bit, Will and Bertie are on their way over with a letter Merlin got here in this morning's post, mad isn't it"

"Very, I'll just let him know, bear with, Merlin? It's Zoe over in Marlborough, she says Bertha's on her way over with Will, seems you received another letter in the post this morning".

"What's his response?" Zoe asked.

"He simply raised an eyebrow, don't think he knows what to think yet, obviously".

"Yeah, I'm dying to find out what's in it".

"Me too, I'll keep you posted, do you and Chris want to come over for drinkies or similar sometime soon?

"Yes please, don't know about you, I'm a bit low this morning because I'm not there, don't get me wrong, I love home, but it was perfect wasn't it?"

"Really was, look, we're all feeling it too, anytime you want, don't need to ask just pop over, kettle is always primed as is the stronger stuff, we should all have a girlie night".

"Oh definitely. You, me, Kelly, Bertha, Katy if she's up for it?
"Done!"

"Brilliant, can't wait, speak to you in a bit, ok?"

"Yes, will do!"

Once Gwen had hung up her phone, Todd remembered he had a letter that had arrived for him too, sat in the kitchen, he left his toast to run and fetch it.

"What you got there, Todd?" Gwen asked.

"Merlin wasn't the only one to get a letter this morning. I had to close it again because I didn't realise it was full of glitter, so I need to open it more carefully this time," Todd replied.

"Hang on, Todd I've got a proper letter opener round here somewhere, that'll make it easier". Dave fetched the letter opener, it was tiny and had a little windmill at the top, even the little sails turned round "Nanny Vicky left this here when she last visited, so we may as well use it. She'd approve I'm sure. Todd took the opener and carefully put the thin end into the end of the envelope, he'd been shown how this worked before, carefully ripping through the top flap of the envelope, he was then able to carefully pull the letter from the envelope sprinkling minimum amounts of glitter on the table.

"It's from Lucy," Todd declared, "how did she know our address?"

"She probably asked Summer, "Noah replied, "or there's magic behind it, bit like when we write to Santa every year, somehow he gets it. And don't forget the elves, there's gonna be a way we don't know about yet". The doorbell rang again.

"Oh that'll be Will and Bertha, "said Gwen.

"On it!" said Dave.

Dave opened the door.

"Hello Dave, " said Will, shaking his hand enthusiastically.

"Hello you two, come on in".

"Hello Dad, " said Bertha upon seeing Merlin at the table tucking into a bowl of crunchy nut cornflakes.

"Hello, darling girl, how are you?" he replied.

"Oh fine, we're popping back over to Oxford, but needed to bring you something on the way"

"Ah yes, the mysterious letter, Gwen and Zoe have already spoken this morning only recently in fact, I was going to pop over to Oxford myself by bus, but made the obvious decision to wait until you had visited".

"Ah okay, well, here it is", Bertha retrieved it from Will's pocket, she didn't have pockets. Merlin took the letter and said, "Todd, may I borrow your grandmother's letter opener? Just in case this is also from the North Pole.

"Yes of course, "said Todd, handing the letter opener over. Merlin took the same care Todd had taken with his letter from Lucy. He needn't have worried, as there was no glitter inside. "Well, " Merlin said, "not from the North Pole but, it is from me, unsurprisingly, the address at the top is Tintagel, interestingly dated 1301 which is 25 years in my future, apologies, I need to study this carefully".

After what felt like hours, Merlin finally stood up and said "right, okay, I think I've figured out what needs to happen, time is irrelevant as in, it doesn't matter when I return to Tintagel because I will be returning to the date that I originally intended, so I shall start by going to Oxford like I said I would but then, I will be going back to Tintagel to take up my original timeline and put a putting right a few errors if I can, wish me luck everyone, Bertha, I shall see you in Oxford, where I intend to remain for a while before going home which I advise you don't join me for but you are welcome to obviously, sorry

I'm being vague, I will try to make things clearer when I see you, another adventure awaits but as always, that is another story!

Epilogue

noun

a section or speech at the end of a book or play that serves as a comment on or a conclusion to what has happened.

An epilogue or epilog is a piece of writing at the end of a work of literature, usually used to bring closure to the work. It is presented from the perspective of within the story. When the author steps in and speaks directly to the reader, that is more properly considered an afterword.

Seems rude not to add a bit more doesn't it?
Well, a few things to mention really.
1. Merlin did indeed have his first cross-country bus adventure to Oxford.
2. Todd wrote back to Lucy the same day, his letter,which as Noah had said it would, arrived with Lucy without any need for an address on the envelope
3. The three boys all got the best christmas present each; an individual door which gave them instant access directly from their bedroom at home to their own pod in the Rainbow Quarter. They also each received a copy of Charles Dickens' "A Christmas Carol"
4. Peter Pan, the lost boys and Tinkerbell made it to Hogwarts successfully though Tink accidentally got

mistaken for a golden snitch in a very turbulent game of quidditch!
5. Dave and Gwen took the boys on an incredible holiday to Florida which gave them their first taste of Disneyland and allowed them time to have a good chat about their winnings.

The Lost Merlin Chronicles - Featured Characters

Just as in the other books, some of the characters in this book were absolutely real, so I thought I would include some details about them. Any characters that don't appear with a description on these following pages can be assumed as purely fictitious without any reference to anyone living or otherwise. Though ask me and I may divulge the inspiration for them. The characters listed here are the most key ones in this book, for more, go to my website and on the menu you can choose 'books' then you will see a list of the books where you can access more things such as links to more information on the characters, images etc etc. There is a scannable qr code near the end of this book which will take you to the "A very Merlin Christmas' web page, or you can
type into a browser www.tobyvennard.co.uk or https://shorturl.at/bczDN

J.M.Barrie

James Matthew Barrie, 1st Baronet.
9 May 1860 – 19 June 1937

...was a Scottish novelist and playwright, best remembered as the creator of Peter Pan. He was born and educated in Scotland and then moved to London, where he wrote several successful novels and plays. There he met the Llewelyn Davies boys, who inspired him to write about a baby boy who has magical adventures in Kensington Gardens (first included in Barrie's 1902 adult novel *The Little White Bird*), then to write *Peter Pan, or The Boy Who Wouldn't Grow Up*, a 1904 West End "fairy play" about an ageless boy and an ordinary girl named Wendy who have adventures in the fantasy setting of Neverland.

Although he continued to write successfully, *Peter Pan* overshadowed his other work, and is credited with popularising the name Wendy. Barrie unofficially adopted the Davies boys following the deaths of their parents. Barrie was made a baronet by King George V on 14 June 1913, and a member of the Order of Merit in the 1922 New Year Honours. Before his death, he gave the rights to the Peter Pan works to Great Ormond Street Hospital for Children in London, which continues to benefit from them.

James Matthew Barrie was born in Kirriemuir, Angus, to a conservative Calvinist family. His father, David Barrie, was a modestly successful weaver. His mother, Margaret Ogilvy, assumed her deceased mother's household responsibilities at the age of eight. Barrie was the ninth child of ten (two of whom died before he was born), all of whom were schooled in at least the three Rs in preparation for possible professional careers. He was a small child and drew attention to himself with storytelling. He grew to only 5 ft $3^1/_2$ in. (161 cm) according to his 1934 passport.

When James Barrie was six years old, his elder brother David (their mother's favourite) died in an ice-skating accident on the day before his 14th birthday. This left his mother devastated, and Barrie tried to fill David's place in his mother's attentions, even wearing David's clothes and whistling in the manner that he did. One time, Barrie entered her room and heard her say, "Is that you?" "I thought it was the dead boy she was speaking to", wrote Barrie in his biographical account of his mother *Margaret Ogilvy* (1896) "and I said in a little lonely voice, 'No, it's no' him, it's just me.'" Barrie's mother found comfort in the fact that her dead son would remain a boy forever, never to grow up and leave her. Eventually, Barrie and his mother entertained each other with stories of her brief childhood and books such as *Robinson Crusoe*, works by fellow Scotsman Walter Scott, and *The Pilgrim's Progress*.

At the age of eight, Barrie was sent to the Glasgow Academy in the care of his eldest siblings, Alexander and Mary Ann, who taught at the school. When he was 10, he returned home and continued his education at the Forfar Academy. At 14, he left home for Dumfries Academy, again under the watch of Alexander and Mary Ann. He became a voracious reader and was fond of penny dreadfuls and the works of Robert Michael Ballantyne and James Fenimore Cooper. At Dumfries, he and his friends spent time in the garden of Moat Brae house, playing pirates "in a sort of Odyssey that was long afterwards to become the play of *Peter Pan*". They formed a drama club, producing his first play *Bandelero the Bandit*, which provoked a minor controversy following a scathing moral denunciation from a clergyman on the school's governing board.

Barrie knew that he wished to follow a career as an author. However, his family attempted to persuade him to choose a profession such as the ministry. With advice from Alexander, he was able to work out a compromise: he would attend a university, but would study literature. Barrie enrolled at the University of Edinburgh where he wrote drama reviews for the *Edinburgh Evening Courant*. He graduated and obtained an M.A. on 21 April 1882.

Charles Dickens

Charles John Huffam Dickens (FRSA) 7 February 1812 – 9 June 1887

Charles Dickens was an English writer and social critic. He created some of the world's best-known fictional characters and is regarded by many as the greatest novelist of the Victorian era. His works enjoyed unprecedented popularity during his lifetime and, by the 20th century, critics and scholars had recognised him as a literary genius. His novels and short stories are widely read today.

Born in Portsmouth, Dickens left school at the age of 12 to work in a factory when his father was incarcerated in a debtors' prison. After three years he was returned to school, before he began his literary career as a journalist. Dickens edited a weekly journal for 20 years, wrote 15 novels, five novellas, hundreds of short stories and non-fiction articles, lectured and performed readings extensively, was an indefatigable letter writer, and campaigned vigorously for children's rights, education and other social reforms.

Dickens's literary success began with the 1836 serial publication of *The Pickwick Papers*, a publishing phenomenon—thanks largely to the introduction of the character Sam Weller in the fourth episode—that sparked *Pickwick* merchandise and spin-offs. Within a few years Dickens had become an international literary celebrity, famous for his humour, satire and keen observation of character and society. His novels, most of them published in monthly or weekly instalments, pioneered the serial publication of narrative fiction, which became the dominant Victorian mode for novel publication. Cliffhanger endings in his serial publications kept readers in suspense. The instalment format allowed Dickens to evaluate his audience's reaction, and he often modified his plot and character development based on such feedback. For example, when his wife's chiropodist expressed distress at the way Miss Mowcher in *David Copperfield* seemed to reflect her disabilities, Dickens improved the character with positive features His plots were carefully constructed and he often wove elements from topical events into his narratives. Masses of the illiterate poor would individually pay a halfpenny to have each new monthly episode read to them, opening up and inspiring a new class of readers.

His 1843 novella *A Christmas Carol* remains especially popular and continues to inspire adaptations in every artistic genre. *Oliver Twist* and *Great Expectations* are also frequently adapted and, like many of his novels, evoke images of early Victorian London. His 1859 novel *A Tale of Two Cities* (set in London and Paris) is his best-known work of historical fiction. The most famous celebrity of his era, he undertook, in response to public demand, a series of public reading tours in the later part of his career. The term *Dickensian* is used to describe something that is reminiscent of Dickens and his writings, such as poor social or working conditions, or comically repulsive characters.

Lewis Carroll

Charles Lutwidge Dodgson
27 January 1832 – 14 January 1898

Better known by his pen name **Lewis Carroll**, was an English writer of children's fiction, notably *Alice's Adventures in Wonderland* and its sequel *Through the Looking-Glass*. He was noted for his facility with word play, logic, and fantasy. The poems "Jabberwocky" and *The Hunting of the Snark* are classified in the genre of literary nonsense. He was also a mathematician, photographer, inventor, and Anglican deacon. Carroll came from a family of high-church Anglicans, and developed a long relationship with Christ Church, Oxford, where he lived for most of his life as a scholar and teacher. Alice Liddell, daughter of the Dean of Christ Church, Henry Liddell, is widely identified as the original for *Alice in Wonderland*, though Carroll always denied this.

In 1982, a memorial stone to Carroll was unveiled in Poets' Corner, Westminster Abbey. There are Lewis Carroll societies in many parts of the world dedicated to the enjoyment and promotion of his works.

Roald Dahl

13 September 1916 – 23 November 1990

Roald Dahl was a British author of popular children's literature and short stories, a poet, and wartime fighter ace. His books have sold more than 300 million copies worldwide. Dahl has been called "one of the greatest storytellers for children of the 20th century".

Dahl was born in Wales to affluent Norwegian immigrant parents, and spent most of his life in England. He served in the Royal Air Force

(RAF) during the Second World War. He became a fighter pilot and, subsequently, an intelligence officer, rising to the rank of acting wing commander. He rose to prominence as a writer in the 1940s with works for children and for adults, and he became one of the world's best-selling authors. His awards for contribution to literature include the 1983 World Fantasy Award for Life Achievement and the British Book Awards' Children's Author of the Year in 1990. In 2008, *The Times* placed Dahl 16th on its list of "The 50 Greatest British Writers Since 1945". In 2021, *Forbes* ranked him the top-earning dead celebrity.

Dahl's short stories are known for their unexpected endings, and his children's books for their unsentimental, macabre, often darkly comic mood, featuring villainous adult enemies of the child characters. His children's books champion the kindhearted and feature an underlying warm sentiment. His works for children include *James and the Giant Peach*, *Charlie and the Chocolate Factory*, *Matilda*, *The Witches*, *Fantastic Mr Fox*, *The BFG*, *The Twits*, *George's Marvellous Medicine* and *Danny, the Champion of the World*. His works for older audiences include the short story collections *Tales of the Unexpected* and *The Wonderful Story of Henry Sugar and Six More*.

Arthur Rackham

19 September 1867 – 6 September 1939

Was an English book illustrator. He is recognised as one of the leading figures during the Golden Age of British book illustration. His work is noted for its robust pen and ink drawings, which were combined with the use of watercolour, a technique he developed due to his background as a journalistic illustrator.

Rackham's 51 colour pieces for the early American tale *Rip Van Winkle* became a turning point in the production of books since – through colour-separated printing – it featured the accurate reproduction of colour artwork. His best-known works also include the illustrations for *Peter Pan in Kensington Gardens*, and *Fairy Tales of the Brothers Grimm*.

Rackham was born at 210 South Lambeth Road, Vauxhall, London as one of 12 children. In 1884, at the age of 17, he was sent on an ocean voyage to Australia to improve his fragile health, accompanied by two aunts. At the age of 18, he worked as an insurance clerk at the Westminster Fire Office and began studying part-time at the Lambeth School of Art.

In 1892, he left his job and started working for the *Westminster Budget* as a reporter and illustrator. His first book illustrations were published in 1893 in *To the Other Side* by Thomas Rhodes, but his first serious commission was in 1894 for *The Dolly Dialogues*, the collected sketches of Anthony Hope, who later went on to write *The Prisoner of Zenda*. Book illustrating then became Rackham's career for the rest of his life.

By the turn of the century, Rackham had developed a reputation for pen and ink fantasy illustration with richly illustrated gift books such as *The Ingoldsby Legends* (1898), *Gulliver's Travels* and *Fairy Tales of the Brothers Grimm* (both 1900). This was developed further through the austere years of the Boer War with regular contributions to children's periodicals such as *Little Folks* and *Cassell's Magazine*. In 1901 he moved to Wychcombe Studios near Haverstock Hill, and in 1903 married his neighbour Edyth Starkie.

Saint Nicholas of Myra

also known as Nicholas of Bari
traditionally 15 March 270 – 6 December 343

Saint Nicholas of Myra (traditionally 15 March 270 – 6 December 343), also known as **Nicholas of Bari**, was an early Christian bishop of Greek descent from the maritime city of Myra in Asia Minor (Greek: Μύρα; modern-day Demre, Turkey) during the time of the Roman Empire. Because of the many miracles attributed to his intercession, he is also known as **Nicholas the Wonderworker**. Saint Nicholas is the patron saint of sailors, merchants, archers, repentant thieves, children, brewers, pawnbrokers, unmarried people, and students in various cities and countries around Europe. His reputation evolved among the pious, as was common for early Christian saints, and his legendary habit of secret gift-giving gave rise to the traditional model of **Santa Claus** ("Saint Nick") through Sinterklaas.

Little is known about the historical Saint Nicholas. The earliest accounts of his life were written centuries after his death and probably contain legendary elaborations. He is said to have been born in the Greek seaport of Patara, Lycia, in Asia Minor to wealthy Christian parents.

Alice Pleasance Hargreaves (*née* Liddell)
4 May 1852 – 16 November 1934

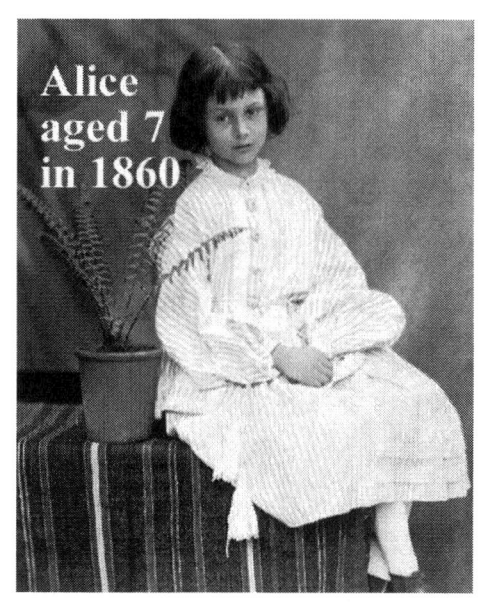

Alice aged 7 in 1860

Alice Pleasance Hargreaves (*née* **Liddell**, 4 May 1852 – 16 November 1934) was an English woman who, in her childhood, was an acquaintance and photography subject of Lewis Carroll. One of the stories he told her during a boating trip became the classic 1865 children's novel *Alice's Adventures in Wonderland*. She shared her name with "Alice", the story's heroine, but scholars disagree about the extent to which the character was based upon her.Alice Liddell was the fourth of the ten children of Henry Liddell, ecclesiastical dean of Christ Church, Oxford, one of the editors of *A Greek-English Lexicon*, and his wife Lorina Hanna Liddell (*née* Reeve). She had two older brothers, Harry (born 1847) and Arthur (1850–53), an older sister Lorina (born 1849) and six younger siblings, including her sister Edith (born 1854) to whom she was very close, and her brother Frederick (born 1865).At the time of her birth, her father was the Headmaster of Westminster School but was soon after appointed to the deanery of Christ Church, Oxford. The Liddell family moved to Oxford in 1856. Soon after this move, Alice met Charles Lutwidge Dodgson (Lewis Carroll), who encountered the family while photographing the cathedral on 25 April 1856. He became a close friend of the Liddell family in subsequent years. Alice was three years younger than Lorina and two years older than Edith, and the three sisters were constant childhood companions. She and her family regularly spent holidays at their holiday home Penmorfa, which later became the Gogarth Abbey Hotel, on the West Shore of Llandudno in North Wales. Alice Liddell married Reginald Hargreaves, a cricketer, on 15 September 1880, at the age of 28 in Westminster Abbey. They had three sons: Alan Knyveton Hargreaves and Leopold Reginald "Rex" Hargreaves (both were killed in action in World War I); and Caryl Liddell Hargreaves, who survived to have a daughter of his own. Liddell denied that the name 'Caryl' was in any way associated with Charles Dodgson's pseudonym. Reginald Hargreaves inherited a considerable fortune, and was a local magistrate; he also played cricket for Hampshire. Alice became a noted society hostess and was the first president of Emery Down Women's Institute.

During World War I, she joined the Red Cross as a volunteer, for which she was awarded a medal.

The Merlin Chronicles Timeline (1.2)
- Revised -

(Version 1 was included at the end of the 2nd book 'Ghost Writers', this is now version 1.2, a revised version which assumes you have read at least the first two books in this collection, it won't contain any spoilers regarding the 3rd book 'Reality Roulette' or indeed this book).

450   Merlin and Ganieda arrive at Tintagel from 2085
1189   Gwendolyn born
1211   Merlin and Gwendolyn Marry
1215   Bertha born
1220   Sir Dave of Cotwolds born
1233   Merlin and Dan travel to Chiseldon to plant apple tree seeds up on the Ridgeway between Suindune (Swindon) and Marlborough.
         Merlin leaves for Swindon of the 21st century
         Merlin returns from the future with his descendents
         Merlin and his descendents return to 21st century Wiltshire
1235   Merlin and Bertha travel to Oxford and meet Kathryn

1242   Sir Dave marries wife
1243   Sir Dave's first son born
1247   Sir Dave's second son is born

1852	4th May	Alice Pleasance Liddell is born
1866	21st September	H.G.Wells is born
1887	H.G.Wells starts his stay at Upark for the winter to convalesce	
1888	January	Merlin meets Wells
	February	Wells travels to the year 2076
1931	The Inklings are formed and initiated by Edward Tangye Lean	

1933 Lean left Oxford, Tolkien and Lewis adopted the name and applied it to their group over at Magdalen college.

1976	February	Modern day Dave born
1998	April 23rd	Chris and Zoe Marry
1999	November 12th	Will is born, (*adopted two months later by Chris and Zoe*)
1999	22nd May	Kathryn born
	9th September	Sam born
2000	6th December	Modern day Dave and Gwen marry
2002	Christmas day	Summer arrives at the North Pole
2011	June	Noah born
2015	April	Todd born

2018 Merlin arrives from the 13th Century in Swindon and the events of "The sleepy dragon" play out.

2018 September Kathryn(*19*) starts college and is visited by Merlin and Bertha and so the events of "Ghost Writers" then plays out.

2036 June Kaelyn(*Merlin and Ganieda's Mother, daughter of Katy and Sam*) is born

2074	August	Ganieda (*Merlin's Sister*) born
2076	June	Merlin is born

2076 Wells visits from the past which goes on to inspire his novel 'The Time Machine'

2085 October Merlin(*9*) and Ganieda(*11*) relocate to the 5th century.

About the author - Toby Vennard.

Born 1976 in Chichester, West Sussex, England. Lives in Bognor Regis, West Sussex, England

Education:
1) Villa Maria convent (primary school), Bognor Regis, West Sussex, England. 1980 - 1985
2) Downview (primary school), Felpham, Bognor Regis, West Sussex, England. 1985 - 1987
3) Felpham Community College (secondary school), Felpham, Bognor Regis, West Sussex, England. 1987 - 1993
4) Northbrook College, Goring-by-sea, Worthing, Sussex, England. 1993 - 1995
5) Chichester college of arts science and technology, Chichester, West Sussex, England. 1995 - 2002

Creative Work:

Musicals:
1) **80 Days - The Musical** (2003) – Original Score / Orchestrations / Musical Arrangements, Additional Lyrics.
2) **Something Wicked** (2005) – Original Score / Orchestrations / Musical Arrangements, Additional Lyrics.
3) **Super** (A musical comedy about the superhuman condition) (2008) Original Score / Orchestrations / Musical Arrangements, Additional Lyrics

Author's other books...

Books as part of the lost Merlin Chronicles

1)Sleepy Dragon
Two young brothers discover they are not only descendants of a famous local knight, but also Merlin. They meet more of their family, and end up having adventures travelling through time to help rescue Merlin's wife and Merlin himself, oh and not forgetting Merlin's pet dragon, will magic and modern technology help save the day without changing the course of history? And what does Alice's looking glass have to do with it? Chuck in a horse, a fox, a badger, a dog, two owls and a family of hedgehogs into the mix, and that should help our heroes on their quest.

2)Ghost Writers
Kathryn has just started at Oxford and wants to become an author but she's got a bad case of writer's block. Will her new friends Bertie and Bertie's Father Merlin be able to help? The noise of voices aren't helping her to focus at all until she learns the voices belong to two of the most famous authors of the 20th century. Many authors from throughout history join the party and team up to help

Kathryn with her problem. To add to the mystery of it all, there has been a murder in the afterlife. But how do you murder someone who is already dead? Merlin's story continues, raising more questions than it answers as we uncover his origins in the future.

3)Reality roulette
As of the date of this list, 'Reality roulette' has not yet been released.

5)In it to win it
As of the date of this list, 'In it to win it' has not yet been released.

Dream a little dream
The story of Kaelyn - Merlin's mother.

Grandfathers at war
An account of two men during world war 2 from two very different perspectives. As of the date of this list, this publication has not yet been released.

Printed in Great Britain
by Amazon